As Caleb entered the Yoder barn, he looked up to see Rebecca coming down the ladder from the hayloft.

She was such a pretty sight, all pink cheeked from the cold, red curls tumbling around her face, and small graceful hands—hands that could bake bread, soothe a crying child and manage a spirited driving horse without hesitation.

"Caleb!" A smile lit her eyes and spread over her face. "I didn't expect you so early."

"*Ya.*" Rebecca often made him trip over his own tongue. "You, too," he added. "Up early."

She nodded. "I like mornings, when it's quiet. A barn can be almost like…like a church. The contented sounds of the animals, the rustle of hay when you throw it down from the loft and…" She broke off, laughing softly. "I must sound foolish."

"*Ne.* I feel the same way…as if God is listening."

When she looked at him, he got the feeling she saw beyond the scars on his face and hand. It was almost as if she didn't see them at all.

Books by Emma Miller

Love Inspired

*Courting Ruth
*Miriam's Heart
*Anna's Gift
*Leah's Choice
*Redeeming Grace
*Johanna's Bridegroom
*Rebecca's Christmas Gift

*Hannah's Daughters

EMMA MILLER

lives quietly in her old farmhouse in rural Delaware amid fertile fields and lush woodlands. Fortunate enough to be born into a family of strong faith, she grew up on a dairy farm, surrounded by loving parents, siblings, grandparents, aunts, uncles and cousins. Emma was educated in local schools, and once taught in an Amish schoolhouse much like the one at Seven Poplars. When she's not caring for her large family, reading and writing are her favorite pastimes.

Rebecca's Christmas Gift

Emma Miller

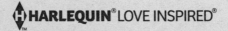

H HARLEQUIN® LOVE INSPIRED®

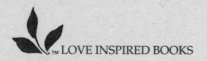 _™ LOVE INSPIRED BOOKS

Recycling programs
for this product may
not exist in your area.

ISBN-13: 978-0-373-87848-2

REBECCA'S CHRISTMAS GIFT

Copyright © 2013 by Emma Miller

www.Harlequin.com

Printed in U.S.A.

"For I know the plans I have for you," declares the Lord, "plans to prosper you and not to harm you, plans to give you hope and a future."
—*Jeremiah* 29:11

Chapter One

Seven Poplars, Kent County, Delaware, Autumn

Rebecca Yoder stole another secret glance at the new preacher before ducking behind an oak tree. Today had been delightful; she couldn't remember when she'd last enjoyed a barn raising so much. Leaning back against the sturdy trunk of the broad-leaved oak, she slipped off her black athletic shoes and wiggled her bare feet in the sweet-smelling clover. It may have been October, but fair weather often lingered late into autumn in Delaware and the earth was still warm under her feet.

She and her friends Mary Byler and Lilly Hershberger had been busy since sunup, cooking, helping to mind the children and squeezing dozens and dozens of lemons to make lemonade for the work frolic. It seemed that half the Amish in the county, and more than a few from out of state, had come to help rebuild new preacher Caleb Wittner's barn, and everyone—from toddlers to white-haired elders—had been hungry.

As adult women, a great deal of the heavy work of feeding people fell to them. Rebecca didn't mind—

she was happy to help—and work frolics were fun. A change from everyday farm chores was always welcome, and gatherings like these gave young people from different church districts an opportunity to meet and socialize. Getting to know eligible men was the first step in courtship, as the eventual goal of every Amish girl was finding a husband.

Not that she would be in the market for one for some time. Technically, at twenty-one, she was old enough to marry, but she liked her life as it was. Her older sisters had all found wonderful husbands, and she intended to take her time and choose the right man. Good men didn't exactly grow on trees, and she wouldn't settle for just anyone. Marriage was for a lifetime and she didn't want to choose in haste. If she couldn't have someone who loved her in a romantic way, she'd remain single.

Rebecca yawned and rubbed the back of her neck. This was the first chance that she, Mary and Lilly, all of courting age, had found to take a break. Here, under the shade trees, they could take a few minutes to relax, talk and enjoy some of the delicious food they'd been serving to the men all afternoon. The fact that their chosen spot was slightly private while offering a perfect view of the young men pulling rotted siding off the old barn was a definite plus.

"I don't care how eligible Caleb Wittner is. I wouldn't want him." Balancing her plate of food, Mary folded her long legs gracefully under her as she lowered herself onto the grass. Her voice dropped to a conspiratorial whisper as she leaned toward Rebecca. "Amish or not, I tell you, I wouldn't set foot in that man's house again, not even for double wages."

Lilly's curly head bobbed in agreement beneath her

spotlessly starched prayer *kapp*. "Didn't I tell you? I warned you before you took the job, Mary. I learned the hard way. He's impossible to please, and that child of his…" Lilly rolled her dark eyes and raised both hands in mock horror, causing a round of mirth. Blonde, round-faced Lilly had a sweet disposition and had been a loyal pal since the three of them had gone to school together as children, but Rebecca knew she was prone to exaggeration.

Actually, Lilly and she had been first graders when they'd met. Mary had been older, but that hadn't stopped her from taking the newcomers under her wing and helping them adjust to being away from their mothers all day. The friendship that had kindled around the school's potbellied woodstove had only grown stronger with each passing year. And since all of them had left their school days behind and become of courting age, not a week went by without the three of them attending a young folks' singing, a trip to Spence's Auction or some sort of frolic together. To cement the bond even more, Mary's brother Charley had married Rebecca's sister Miriam, which made kinship an added blessing. So tight was hers and Mary's friendship that Rebecca often worried how she'd stand it if she married out of the community and had to move away.

"Seriously." Rebecca nibbled at a stuffed egg and returned to the subject of Caleb Wittner's mischievous daughter. "She's a four-year-old. How bad could she be?"

"Oh, she's pretty awful." Mary chuckled as she tucked a stray lock of fine, honey-brown hair behind her ear. "Don't let those big, innocent eyes fool you. Turn your back on that girl and she's stuffing a dead mouse in your apron pocket and tying knots in your shoestrings."

"Together," Lilly added with a grimace. "She tied my church shoes together so tight I had to cut the laces to get them apart. And while I was trying to sort them out, she dumped a crock of honey on the sermon her father had been writing."

"I think you two are being uncharitable," Rebecca pronounced. She eyed one of Aunt Martha's famous pickled carrots on her plate. "And letting your imaginations run away with you." Her attempt at reining in her friends' criticism of Caleb and Amelia Wittner was spoiled by another giggle that she couldn't contain. Mary was terrified of mice. Rebecca could just picture Mary's face when she'd slipped a hand into her pocket and come up with a dead rodent.

"That's not the half of it," Mary went on. "Amelia's impossible, but her father…" She pursed her lips. "He's worse. Short-tempered. Never a kind word for me when I came to watch his daughter. Have you ever seen him smile? Even at church? It's a wonder his face doesn't freeze in winter. He—" Mary broke off abruptly and her face flushed. "I didn't mean…" She shook her head. "I wasn't mocking his scars."

"I didn't think you were," Rebecca assured her. The three of them fell silent for a minute or two, and even Rebecca, who hadn't been critical of the new preacher, felt a little guilty. Caleb had suffered a terrible burn in the fire that had killed his wife. One side of his face was perfectly acceptable, pleasant-looking even, but the other… And his left hand… She shivered. God's mercy had saved him and little Amelia, but had left Caleb a marked man. She swallowed the lump rising in her throat. Who could blame him if he was morose and sad?

"Ya." Lilly took a small bite of fried chicken and went on talking. "It's true that Caleb Wittner is a grouch. And it's not uncharitable to speak the truth about someone. He's nothing like our old Preacher Perry. I miss him."

"We all do." Rebecca sipped at her lemonade, wondering if she'd made it too tart for most people. She liked it as she liked most things—with a bit of a bite. "Preacher Perry always had a joke or a funny story for everyone. What is that English expression? His cup was always full?"

Perry's sudden heart attack and subsequent passing had been a shock to the whole community, but nothing like the surprise of having newcomer Caleb Wittner selected, within weeks of his arrival in Seven Poplars, to take his place as preacher. The position was for life, and his role as shepherd of their church would affect each and every one of them.

"You have to admit that Caleb and Amelia have certainly livened things up in the neighborhood," Rebecca added.

The coming of the new preacher was the most exciting thing that had happened in Seven Poplars since Grace—Rebecca's secret half sister—had appeared on their back porch in a rainstorm two years ago.

Without being obvious, she glanced back at the barn, hoping to catch another glimpse of her new neighbor. There were two men pulling a large piece of rotten sideboard down; one was Will Stutzman, easy to recognize by his purple shirt, and the other was her brother-in-law, John Hartman, Grace's husband. Caleb Wittner was nowhere in sight. Disappointed, she finished the last few bites of her potato salad and rose to her feet. "We better get back and help clear away the desserts before someone comes looking for us."

Her friends stood up, as well. "I wonder if there's any of your sister Anna's *apfelstrudel* left?" Lilly said. "I think I could make room for just one slice."

More than two hours later, as the purple shadows of twilight settled over Caleb's farmstead, Rebecca returned to the trees near the barn to retrieve her shoes. Most of the families who'd come to work and visit had already packed up and gone home. Only a few of those who lived nearby, including her sisters Miriam and Ruth, and their husbands remained. Rebecca had been ready to go when she realized that she was still barefoot; she'd had to stop and think where and when she'd removed her sneakers.

"I remember where they are now," she said to her mother, Hannah, who was just climbing into their buggy. "You and Susanna go on home. I'll go fetch my shoes and see you there." Home was around the corner and across the street. She could just walk.

Mam and Susanna waved and their buggy rolled down the driveway, followed by her sisters and brothers-in-law behind them.

"You want us to wait?" Miriam called as Charley brought their wagon around to head down the driveway.

"I'm fine." Rebecca waved. "See you tomorrow!" As the sun set, she turned to go in search of her shoes.

The barn stood some distance from Caleb's home, which was a neat story-and-a-half 1920s-era brick house. English people had remodeled the house over the years, but had left the big post-and-beam barn to slowly fall into disrepair. Although the roof and siding had deteriorated, the frame of the barn remained sound.

It was the potential of the barn and outbuildings that had drawn Caleb to the ten-acre property, according to Rebecca's brother-in-law Eli. Even though it was quickly getting dark, Rebecca had no problem finding her shoes. They were lying by the tree, exactly as she'd left them. She thrust her foot into the left one and was just lacing it up when she heard a pitiful meow. She glanced around. It sounded like a cat…. No, not a cat, a kitten. Rebecca held her breath and listened, trying to locate the source of the distressed animal. She hadn't seen any cats on the property today. In fact, when she'd been serving at the first meal seating, she'd distinctly heard Caleb say that he didn't like cats.

That had been a strike against him. Rebecca had always liked cats better than dogs. Cats were… They were independent. They didn't give affection lightly, but once they'd decided that you were to be trusted, they could be a great source of company. And they kept a house free of mice. Rebecca had always believed cats to be smart, and there was nothing like a purring cat curled up in her lap at the end of a long day to soothe her troubles and put her in the right mind for prayer.

Meow. The plaintive cry of distress came again, louder than before. It was definitely a kitten; the sound was coming from the shadowy barn. As Rebecca stepped into her other shoe, she glanced in the direction of the house and yard, then back at the barn. Maybe the mother was out hunting and had left a nest of little ones in a safe spot. One of the kittens could have wandered away from the others and gotten lost.

Mee-oo-www.

That settled it. There was no way that she could go home and abandon the little creature without investigation. Otherwise, she'd lie awake all night worrying if it was injured or in danger. Shoes tied, she strode across the leaf-strewn ground toward the barn.

Today hadn't been a proper barn raising because the men hadn't built a new barn; they'd stripped the old one to a shell. Tomorrow the men would return, accompanied by a volunteer group from the local Mennonite church and other Amish men who hadn't been able to take a Friday off. They'd nail up new exterior siding and put on a roof. The Amish women would return at noon with a hearty lunch and supper for the workers.

Rebecca looked up at the barn that loomed skeleton-like in the semidarkness. She wasn't easily scared, but heavy shadows already lay deep in the structure's interior, and she wished she'd thought to come back for her shoes earlier.

She stepped over a pile of fresh lumber and listened again. This time it was easy to tell that a kitten was crying, and it was coming from above her head. Only one section of the old loft floor remained; the planks were unsound and full of holes. The rest was open space all the way to the roof, two stories above, divided by beams. Tomorrow, men would tear out the rest of the old floor, toss down the rotten wood to be burned and hammer down new boards.

Meow.

Rebecca glanced dubiously at the wooden ladder leaning against the interior hall framing. Darkness had already settled over the interior of the barn. It was difficult to see more than a few feet, but she could see well enough to know that there was no solid floor above her.

The sensible thing would be to leave and return in the morning. By then, the mother cat would probably have returned for her kitten and the problem would be solved. At the very least, Rebecca knew she should walk back to Caleb's house to get a flashlight.

But what if the kitten fell? Nine lives or not, the loft was a good fourteen feet from the concrete floor. The baby couldn't survive such trauma. And what if it got cold tonight? It was already much cooler than it had been this afternoon when the sun was shining. She didn't know if the kitten could survive a night without its mama. What she *did* know was that she didn't have the heart to abandon the kitten. Making up her mind, she started up the ladder.

Caleb tucked his sleeping daughter into bed; it was early for bedtime, but she'd had a long day. He covered her with a light blanket and placed her rag doll under her arm. He never picked it up without a lump of sadness tightening in his throat. Dinah had sewn the doll for Amelia before the child was born. It was small and soft and stuffed with quilt batting. Dinah's skillful fingers had placed every stitch with love and skill, and Baby, with her blank face and tangled hair, was Amelia's most cherished possession.

He paused to push a lock of dark hair off the child's forehead. Amelia had crawled up into the rocking chair and fallen asleep when Caleb was seeing the last of his neighbors off. He hadn't even had time to bathe her before carrying her upstairs to the small, whitewashed room across the hall from his own bedchamber. A mother would likely wake a drowsy child to wash her and put her in a clean nightgown before putting her to bed, but there was no mother.

It seemed to Caleb that a sleeping child ought to be left to sleep in peace. It was only natural that active *kinner* got dirty in the course of a busy day. Morning would be good enough for soap and water before breakfast.

"God keep you," he murmured, turning away from the bed. To the dog standing in the doorway, he said, "Fritzy. *Bescherm!*" Obediently, the black Standard Poodle dropped to a sitting position and fixed his attention on Amelia.

Absently, Caleb's hand rose to stroke the gnarled side of his face where only a sparse and ragged beard grew. The burned flesh that had pained him so fiercely in the days after the fire had finally healed. Now he had no feeling in the area at all.

Some said that he'd been lucky that his mouth hadn't been twisted, that his speech remained much as it had always been, but Caleb didn't agree. Luck would have been reaching his wife before the smoke had claimed her life. Luck would have been that Dinah and he and Amelia could have built a new home and continued their lives as before. A small voice whispered from the far corner of his consciousness that he asked too much of God, that the blessing had been that his daughter had come out of that inferno alive.

He did not blame God. The fire that had consumed their farmhouse had been an accident. A gust of wind… A spark from a lamp. The cause was never truly determined, but as Caleb saw it, the fault, if there was fault, had been his. He had not protected his family, and his precious wife had been lost to him and his beloved child.

"Watch over her," he ordered the dog. With Fritzy on duty, Caleb was free to check that his horse was safe, that the toolshed doors were locked and that all was secure.

Flat, green Delaware was a long way from the dry highlands of Idaho and the Old Order Amish community that he'd left behind. After the fire and the death of his wife, Caleb had tried to do as his bishop had urged. He'd tried to pick up his life and carry on for the sake of his child. He'd even gone so far as to consider, after a year, courting a plump widow with a kind face who belonged to his church. But the bitter memories of his past had haunted him and he'd decided to try to pick up the pieces of his life somewhere new. In Idaho, there had been no family ties to hold him. Here, where his cousin Eli lived, things might be better. It had to be good for Amelia to grow up with relatives, and Eli's wife had six sisters. A woman's hand was what Amelia needed, he told himself.

Caleb left the kitchen and walked out into the yard. All was quiet. His house was far enough off the road that he wasn't bothered by the sounds of passing traffic. There were several sheds and a decent stable for the horse. The old barn, a survivor from earlier times than the house, stood farther back. Caleb was pleased with the work that had been done on it today. Alone, it would have taken him months. There were good people here, people that he instinctively knew he could trust. He prayed to God that this move to Delaware had been the right one for both him and Amelia.

He walked on a little farther, drawn by the sweet scent of new wood that lay stacked, ready and waiting for the following day. He stood for a moment in the semidarkness and gazed up at the exposed beams. He thought about the laughter and the camaraderie during their work today. Everyone had been kind to him and Amelia, trying to make them feel welcome. And he *had* felt welcome…but he hadn't felt as if he was part of the community. He still felt like an outsider, looking in through a glass-paned window, hearing their laughter but not feeling it. And he so *wanted* to feel laughter again.

Caleb was about to turn back to the house when he heard a thud and then a clatter from the barn. Something had fallen or been knocked over inside the building. Had some animal wandered in? Or did he have a curious intruder? "Who's there?" he called as he approached the open front wall.

"Just me," came a woman's voice from high above.

Caleb stepped inside and looked up to see a shadowy form swaying on a loft floor beam. A sense of panic went through him and he raised both hands. "Stop! Don't move!"

"I'm fine. I just—" Her foot slipped and she swayed precariously, arms outstretched, before recovering her balance.

Caleb gasped. "Stay where you are," he ordered. "I'm coming up."

"I'll be fine." She lowered herself down onto the beam until she was kneeling. "It's just hard to see. Do you have a flashlight?"

"What in the name of common sense are you doing in my loft, woman?" He ran for the ladder and climbed it at double speed. "*Ne!* Don't move."

"I don't need your help," she said, taking a sassy tone

with him. Rising to her feet again, she began traversing the beam toward him.

"I told you to stay put!" Caleb had never been afraid of heights, but he was all too aware of the distance to the concrete floor and the possibility of serious injury or death if one or both of them fell. He stood cautiously, finding his balance, then stepped slowly toward her.

"Go back," she insisted. "I can do this."

"*Ya,* maybe you can," he answered gruffly. "Or maybe you can't, and I'll have to scrape you up off my barn floor with a shovel." He quickly closed the distance between them, reached out and swept her up in his arms.

Chapter Two

Caleb carried Rebecca to the end of the crossbeam and set her securely on the ladder. "You got your balance?"

Her hands tightened on the rung and she found solid footing under her before answering. "I'm fine. I really could have managed the beam." She slipped into the Pennsylvania *Deitsch* dialect that was their first language. "I wasn't going to fall." It wasn't as if she hadn't climbed the loft ladder in her father's barn a thousand times without ever slipping. Nimbly, she made her way down the ladder to the barn floor and stepped aside to allow him to descend.

"It didn't look like you were *managing*. You nearly fell off before I got to you."

A sharp reply rose in Rebecca's mind, but she pressed her lips together and swallowed it. Caleb Wittner's coming to her rescue, or what he'd obviously *believed* was coming to her rescue, was almost… It was… Her lips softened into a smile. It was as romantic as a hero coming to the rescue of a maiden in a story. He'd thought she was in danger and he'd put himself in harm's way to save her. It didn't matter that she wasn't *really* in danger. *"Danke,"* she murmured. "I'm sorry if I caused you trouble."

"You should be sorry."

His words were stern without being harsh. Caleb was obviously upset with her, but his was the voice of a take-charge and reasonable man. Somehow, even though he was scolding her, Rebecca found something pleasant and reassuring in his tone. He was almost a stranger, yet, oddly, she felt as though she could trust him.

Meow.

"Vas ist das?"

"Ach." In the excitement of having Caleb rescue her, she'd almost forgotten her whole reason for being in the barn in the first place. "It's a *katzenbaby*," she exclaimed as she drew the little creature out of the bodice of her dress. "A kitten," she said, switching back to English and crooning softly to it. "Shh, shh, you're safe now." And to Caleb she said, "It's tiny. Probably hasn't had its eyes open long."

"A cat? You climbed up to the top of my barn in the dark for a *katzen?*"

"A baby." She kissed the top of the kitten's head. It was as soft as duckling down. "I think the poor little thing has lost its mother. It was crying so loudly, I just couldn't abandon it." She raised the kitten to her cheek and heard the crying change from a pitiful mewing to a purr. The kitten nuzzled against her and Rebecca felt the scratchy surface of a small tongue against her skin. "It must be hungry."

"Everyone has left for the night," he said, ignoring the kitten. "What are you still doing here?"

Rebecca sighed. "I forgot my *schuhe.* I'd taken off my sneakers while…" She sensed his impatience and finished her explanation in a rush of words. "I left my shoes under the tree when I went to serve the late meal. And when I came to fetch them, I heard the kitten in distress." She cradled the little animal in her hands and it burrowed between her fingers. "Why do you think the mother cat moved the others and left this one behind?"

"There are no cats here. I've no use for cats," he said gruffly. "I have no idea how this one got in my loft."

Caleb's English was excellent, although he did have a slightly different accent in *Deitsch*. She didn't think she'd ever met anyone from Idaho. He was Eli's cousin, but Eli had grown up in Pennsylvania.

He loomed over her. "Come to the house. My daughter is in bed, but I'll wake her, hitch up my horse and drive you home. Where do you live?"

Rebecca felt a pang of disappointment; she'd assumed he knew who she was. She supposed that it was too dark for Caleb to make out her face now. Still, she'd hoped that he'd taken enough notice of her in church or elsewhere in the daylight to recognize her by her voice. "I'm Rebecca. Rebecca Yoder. One of Eli's wife's sisters."

"Not the youngest one. What's her name? The girl with the sweet smile. Susanna. Her, I remember. You must be the next oldest." He took her arm and guided her carefully out of the building. "Watch your step," he cautioned.

The moon was just rising over the trees, but she still couldn't see his face clearly. His fingers were warm but rough against her bare skin. For the first time, she felt uncertain and a little breathless. "I'm fine," she said, pulling away from him.

"Your mother will not be pleased that you didn't

leave with the others," he said. "It's not seemly for us to be alone after nightfall."

"I'm not so young that my mother expects me to be in the house by dark." She wanted to tell him that he should know who she was, that she was a baptized member of his church and not a silly girl, but she didn't. "Speak in haste, repent at leisure," her *grossmama* always said.

Honestly, she could understand how Caleb might have been startled to find an intruder in his barn after dark. And it was true that it was awkward, her being here after everyone else had already left. She wasn't ready to judge him for being short with her.

"It's kind of you to offer," she said, using a gentler voice. "But I don't need you to take me home. And it would be foolish to get Amelia—" she let him know that she was familiar with his daughter's name, even if he didn't know hers "—to wake a sleeping child to drive me less than a mile. I'm quite capable of walking home." She hesitated. "But what do I do about the kitten? Shall I take it with me or—"

"*Ya.* Take the *katzen.* If it stays here, being so young, it will surely die."

"But if the mother returns for it and finds it gone—"

"Rebecca, I said I haven't seen a cat. Why someone didn't find this kitten earlier when we were working on the loft floor, I don't know. Now let me hitch my buggy. Eli would be—"

"I told you, I don't need your help," she answered firmly. "Eli would agree with me, as would my mother." With that, she turned her back on him and strode away across the field.

"Rebecca, wait!" he called after her. "You're being unreasonable."

"Good night, Caleb." She kept walking. She'd be home before Mam wound the hall clock and have the kitten warm and fed in two shakes of a lamb's tail.

Caleb stared after the girl as she strode away. It wasn't right that she should walk home alone in the dark. She should have listened to him. He was a man, older than she was and a preacher in her church. She should have shown him more respect.

Rebecca Yoder had made a foolish choice to fetch the kitten and risk harm. Worse, she'd caused him to make the equally foolish decision to go out on that beam after her. He clenched his teeth, pushing back annoyance and the twinge of guilt that he felt. What if the young woman came to harm between here and her house? But what could he do? He couldn't leave Amelia alone in the house to run after Rebecca. Not only would he be an irresponsible father, but he would look foolish.

As foolish as he must have looked carrying that girl.

The memory of walking the beam with Rebecca in his arms rose in his mind and he pushed it away. He hadn't felt the softness of a woman's touch for a long time. Had he been unnecessarily harsh with Rebecca because somewhere, deep inside, he'd been exhilarated by the experience?

Caleb sighed. God's ways were beyond the ability of men and women to understand. He hadn't asked to be a leader of the church, and he certainly hadn't wanted it.

He hadn't been here more than a few weeks and had attended only two regular church Sundays when one of the two preachers died and a new one had to be chosen from among the adult men. The Seven Poplars church used the Old Order tradition of choosing the new preacher by lot. A Bible verse was placed in a hymnal, and the hymnal was added to a pile of hymnals. Those men deemed eligible by the congregation had to, guided by God, choose a hymnal. The man who chose the book with the scripture inside became the new preacher, a position he would hold until death or infirmity prevented him from fulfilling the responsibility. To everyone's surprise, the lot had fallen to him, a newcomer, something that had never happened before to anyone's knowledge. If there was any way he could have refused, he would have. But short of moving away or giving up his faith and turning Mennonite, there was no alternative. The Lord had chosen him to serve, so serve he must.

Caleb looked up at his house, barely visible in the darkness, and came to a halt. He had come to Seven Poplars in the belief that God had led him here. He believed that God had a purpose for him, as He did for all men. What that purpose was, he didn't know, but for the first time since he'd arrived, he felt a calm fall over him. Everyone had said that, with time, the ache he felt in his heart for the loss of his wife would ease, that he would find contentment again.

As he stood there gazing toward his new house— toward his new life—it seemed to Caleb that a weight gradually lifted from his shoulders. "All over a kitten," he murmured aloud, smiling in spite of himself. "More nerve than common sense, that girl." He shook his head, and his wry smile became a chuckle. "If the other females in my new church are as headstrong and unpredictable as she is, heaven help me."

* * *

The following morning, Rebecca and her sisters Miriam, Ruth and Grace walked across the pasture to their sister Anna's house on the neighboring farm. Mam, Grace and Susanna were already there, as they had driven over in the buggy after breakfast. Also present in Anna's sunny kitchen were Cousin Dorcas, their grandmother Lovina—who lived with Anna and her husband, Samuel—and neighbors Lydia Beachy and Fannie Byler. Fortunately, Anna's home was large enough to provide ample space for all the women and a noisy assortment of small children, including Anna's baby, Rose, and Ruth's twins, the youngest children, who'd been born in midsummer.

The women were in the kitchen preparing a noonday meal for the men working on Caleb's barn, and Rebecca had just finished quietly relaying the story of her new kitten's rescue to her sisters.

Rebecca had spent most of the night awake, trying to feed the kitten goat's milk from a medicine dropper with little success. But this morning, Miriam had solved the problem by tucking the orphan into the middle of a pile of nursing kittens on her back porch. The mother cat didn't seem to mind the visitor, so Rebecca's kitten was now sound asleep on Miriam's porch with a full tummy.

Grace fished a plastic fork out of a cup on the table, tasted Fannie's macaroni salad and chuckled. "I'd love to have seen that preacher carrying you and the kitten across that beam," she teased. And then she added, "Hmm, needs salt, I think."

"Keep your saltshaker away from my macaroni salad," Fannie warned good-naturedly from across the room. "Roman has high blood pressure, and I've cut him off salt. If anyone wants it, they can add it at the table."

Grossmama rose out of her rocker and came over to the table where bowls of food for the men were laid out. "A little salt never hurt anyone," she grumbled. "I've been eating salt all my life. Roman works hard. He never got high blood pressure from salt." She peered suspiciously at the blue crockery bowl of macaroni salad. "What are those green things in there?"

"Olives, Grossmama," Anna explained. "Just a few for color. Would you like to taste it?" She offered her a saucer and a plastic fork. "And maybe a little of Ruth's baked beans?"

"Just a little," Grossmama said. "You know I never want to be a bother."

Rebecca met Grace's gaze and it was all the two of them could do not to smile. Grossmama, a widow, had come to live in Kent County when her health and mind had begun to fail. Never an easy woman to deal with, Grossmama still managed to voice her criticism of her daughter-in-law. Their grandmother could be critical and outspoken, but it didn't keep any of them from feeling responsible for her or from loving her.

A mother spent a lifetime caring for others. How could any person of faith fail to care for an elderly relative? And how could they consider placing one of their own in a nursing home for strangers to care for? Rebecca intimately knew the problems of pleasing and watching over her grandmother. She and her sister Leah had spent months in Ohio with her before the family had finally convinced her to give up her home and move East. Still, it was a wonder and a blessing to Rebecca and everyone else that Grossmama—who could be so difficult—had settled easily and comfortably into life with Anna. Sweet and capable Anna, the Yoder sisters felt, had "the touch."

Lydia carried a basket of still-warm-from-the-oven loaves of rye bread to the counter. She was a willowy middle-aged woman, the mother of fifteen children and a special friend of Mam's. "I hope this will be enough," she said. "I had another two loaves in the oven, but the boys made off with one and I needed another for our supper."

"This should be fine," Mam replied. "Rebecca, would you hand me that bread knife and the big cutting board? I'll slice if you girls will start making sandwiches."

Lydia picked up the conversation she, Fannie and Mam had been having earlier, a conversation Rebecca hadn't been able to stop herself from eavesdropping on, since it had concerned Caleb Wittner.

"I don't know what's to be done. Mary won't go back and neither will Lilly. I spoke to Saul's Mary about her girl, Flo, but she's already taken a regular job at Spence's Market in Dover," Fannie said. "Saul's Mary said she imagined our new preacher would have to do his own laundry because not a single girl in the county will consider working for him now that he's run Mary and Lilly off."

"Well, someone has to help him out," Fannie said. She was Eli Lapp's aunt by marriage, and so she was almost a distant relative of Caleb. Thus, she considered herself responsible for helping her new neighbor and preacher. She'd been watching his daughter off and on since Caleb had arrived, but what with her own children and tending the customer counter in the chair shop as well as running the office there, Fannie had her hands full.

Mam arched a brow wryly as she took a fork from the cup and had a taste of one of the salads on the table. "A handful that little one is. I'd take her myself, but she's too young for school." Mam was the teacher at the Seven Poplars schoolhouse. "My heart goes out to a motherless child."

"No excuse for allowing her to run wild," Grossmama put in. "Train up a child the way they should go." This was one of their grandmother's good days, Rebecca decided. Other than asking where her dead son Jonas was, she'd said nothing amiss this morning. Jonas was Grossmama's son, Mam's husband and father to Rebecca and all her sisters. But although Dat had been dead for nearly five years, her grandmother had yet to accept it. Usually, Grossmama claimed that Dat was in the barn, milking the cows, although some days, she was certain that Anna's husband Samuel was Jonas and this was his house and farm, not Samuel Mast's.

"Amelia needs someone who can devote time to her," Fannie agreed. "I wish I could do more, but I tried having her in the office and…" She shook her head. "It just didn't work out. For either of us."

Rebecca grabbed a fork and peered into a bowl of potato salad that had plenty of hard-boiled eggs and paprika, just the way she liked it. From what she'd heard from Mam, Amelia was a terror. Fannie had gone to call Roman to the phone and the little girl had spilled a glass of water on a pile of receipts, tried to cut up the new brochures and stapled everything in sight.

"Caleb Wittner needs our help," Mam said, handing Rebecca a small plate. "He can hardly support himself and his child, tend to church business and cook and clean for himself."

"You should get him a wife," Grossmama said. "I'll have a little of that, too." She pointed to the coleslaw. "A preacher should have a wife."

Lydia and Mam exchanged glances and Mam's lips twitched. She gave her mother-in-law a spoon of the coleslaw on her plate. "We can't just *get him a wife,* Lovina."

"Either a housekeeper or a wife will do," Fannie said. "But one way or another, this can't wait. We have to find someone suitable."

"But who?" Anna asked. "Who would dare after the fuss he and his girl have caused?"

"Maybe we should send Rebecca," Grace suggested.

Rebecca paused, a forkful of Anna's potato salad halfway to her mouth. "Me?"

Her mother looked up from the bowl she was recovering with plastic wrap. "What did you say, Grace?"

Miriam chuckled and looked slyly at Rebecca. "Grace thinks that Rebecca should go."

"To marry Caleb Wittner?" Grossmama demanded. "I didn't hear any banns cried. My hearing's not gone yet."

Anna glanced at Rebecca. "Would you consider it, Rebecca? After…" She rolled her eyes. "You know…the kitten incident." Anna's round face crinkled in a grin.

Rebecca shrugged, then took a bite of potato salad. "Maybe. With only me and Susanna at home, and now that Anna has enough help, why shouldn't I be earning money to help out?"

"You can't marry him without banns," Grossmama insisted, waving her plastic fork. "Maybe that's the way they do it where he comes from. Not here, and not in Ohio. And you are wrong to marry a preacher."

"Why?" Mam asked mildly. "Why couldn't our Rebecca be a preacher's wife?"

"I didn't agree to *marry* him," Rebecca protested, deciding to try a little of the pasta salad at the end of the table. "I didn't even say I'd take the job as housekeeper. Maybe."

"You should try it," Anna suggested.

Rebecca looked to her sister. "You think?" She hesitated. "I suppose I could try it."

"*Gut.* It's settled, then," Fannie pronounced, clapping her hands together.

"*Narrisch,*" her grandmother snapped. "Rebecca can't be a preacher's wife."

"I'm *not* marrying him, Grossmama," Rebecca insisted.

"You're going to be sor-ry," Ruth sang. "If that little mischief-maker Amelia doesn't drive you off, you and Caleb Wittner will be butting heads within the week."

"Maybe," Rebecca said thoughtfully, licking her plastic fork. "And maybe not."

Chapter Three

Two days later, Caleb awoke to a dark and rainy Monday morning. He pushed back the patchwork quilt, shivered as the damp air raised goose bumps on his bare skin and peered sleepily at the plain black clock next to his bed. *"Ach!"* Late… He was late, this morning of all mornings.

He scrambled out of bed and fumbled for his clothes. He had a handful of chores to do before leaving for the chair shop. He had to get Amelia up, give her a decent breakfast and make her presentable. He had animals to feed. He'd agreed to meet Roman Byler at nine, in time to meet the truck that would be delivering his power saws and other woodworking equipment. Roman and Eli had offered to help him move the equipment into the space Caleb was renting from Roman. He'd never been a man who wanted to keep anyone waiting, and he didn't know Roman that well. Not only was Roman a respected member of the church, but he was Eli's partner. What kind of impression would Caleb make on Roman and Eli if he was late his first day of work?

Caleb yanked open the top drawer of the oak dresser

where his clean socks should have been, then remembered they'd all gone into the wash. Laundry was not one of his strong points. He remembered that darks went in with darks, but washing clothes was a woman's job. After four years of being on his own, he still struggled with the chore.

When confronted with a row of brightly colored containers of laundry detergent in the store, all proclaiming to be the best, he always grabbed the nearest. Bleach, he'd discovered, was not his friend, and neither was the iron. He was getting good at folding clothes when he took them off the line, but he'd learned to live with wrinkles.

Socks were his immediate problem. He'd done two big loads of wash on Friday, but the clean clothes had never made it from the laundry basket in the utility room back upstairs to the bedrooms. "Amelia," he called. "Wake up, buttercup! Time to get up!" Sockless, Caleb pulled on one boot and looked around for the other. Odd. He always left both standing side by side at the foot of his bed. *Always*.

He got down on his knees and looked under the bed. No boot. *Where could the other one have gone?*

Amelia, he had already decided, could wear her Sunday dress this morning. That, at least, was clean. Fannie had been kind enough to help with Amelia sometimes, and Caleb had hoped that he could impose on her again today. The least he could do was bring her a presentable child.

"Amelia!" He glanced down the hallway and saw, at once, that her bedroom door was closed. He always left it open—just as he always left his shoes where he could find them easily in the morning. If the door was closed, it hadn't closed itself. "Fritzy?" No answering bark.

Caleb smelled mischief in the air. He hurried to the door, opened it and glanced into Amelia's room. Her bed was empty—her covers thrown back carelessly. And there was no dog on watch.

"Amelia! Are you downstairs?" Caleb took the steps, two at a time.

His daughter had always been a handful. Even as a baby, she hadn't been easy; she'd always had strong opinions about what she wanted and when she wanted it. It was almost as if an older, shrewder girl lurked behind that innocent child's face and those big, bright eyes, eyes so much like his. But there the similarity ended, as he had been a thoughtful boy, cautious and logical. And he had never dared to throw the tantrums Amelia did when things didn't go her way.

Caleb reached the bottom of the stairs and strode into the kitchen, where—as he'd suspected—he found Amelia, Fritzy and trouble. Amelia was *helping out* in the kitchen again.

"Vas ist das?" he demanded, taking in the ruins of what had been a fairly neat kitchen when he'd gone to bed last night.

"Staunen erregen!" Amelia proclaimed. "To surprise you, Dat."

Pancakes or biscuits, Caleb wasn't certain what his daughter had been making. Whatever it was had taken a lot of flour. And milk. And eggs. And honey. A puddle of honey on the table had run over the edge and was dripping into a pile of flour on the floor. Two broken eggs lay on the tiles beside the refrigerator.

"You don't cook without me!"

Fritzy's ears pricked up as he caught sight of the eggs. That's when Caleb realized the dog had been gulping down a plate of leftover ham from Saturday's midday meal that the neighborhood women had provided. He'd intended to make sandwiches with the ham for his lunch.

"Stay!" Caleb ordered the dog as he grabbed a dishcloth and scooped up the eggs and shells.

"I didn't cook," Amelia protested. "I was waiting for you to start the stove." Her lower lip trembled. "But… but my pancakes spilled."

They had apparently spilled all over Amelia. Her hands, face and hair were smeared with white, sticky goo.

Then Caleb spotted his boot on the floor in front of the sink…filled with water. He picked up his boot in disbelief and tipped it over the sink, watching the water go down the drain.

"For Fritzy!" she exclaimed. "He was thirsty and the bowls was dirty."

They were dirty, all right. Every dish he owned had apparently been needed to produce the floury glue she was calling pancakes. "And where are my *socken?*" he demanded, certain now that Amelia's mischief hadn't ended with his soggy boot. He could see the wicker basket was overturned. There were towels on the floor and at least one small dress, but not a sock in sight.

"Crows," Amelia answered. "In our corn. I chased them."

Her muddy nightshirt and dirty bare feet showed that she'd been outside already. In the rain.

"You went outside without me?"

Amelia stared at the floor. One untidy pigtail seemed

coated in a floury crust. "To chase the crows. Out of the corn."

"But what has that to do with my socks?"

"I threw them at the crows, Dat."

"You took my *socken* outside and threw them into the cornfield?"

"*Ne,* Dat." She shook her head so hard that the solid cone of flour paste on her head showered flour onto her shoulders. "From upstairs. From my bedroom window. I threw the sock balls at the crows there."

"And then you went outside?"

"*Ya.*" She nodded. "The sock balls didn't scare 'em away, so Fritzy and me chased 'em with a stick."

"What possessed you to make our clean socks into balls in the first place? And to throw them out the window?" Caleb shook his finger at her for emphasis but knew as he uttered the words what she would say.

"You did, Dat. You showed me how."

He sighed. And so he had. Sometimes when he and Amelia were alone on a rainy or snowy day and bored, he'd roll their clean socks into balls and they'd chase each other through the house, lobbing *socken* at each other. But it had never occurred to him that she would throw the socks out the window. "Upstairs! To your room," he said in his sternest father's voice. He could go without his noonday meal today, and the mess in the kitchen could be cleaned up tonight, but the animals still had to be fed. And Amelia had to be bathed and fed and dressed before he took her with him.

Amelia burst into tears. "But…but I wanted to help."

"Upstairs!"

And then, after the wailing girl fled up the steps, he looked around the kitchen again and realized that his worst fears had come to fruition. He was a failure as a father. He had waited too long to take another wife. This small female was too much for him to manage without a helpmate.

"Lord, help me," he murmured, carrying a couple of dirty utensils to the sink. "What do I do?"

He was at his wit's end. Although he loved Amelia dearly, he didn't think he was an overly indulgent parent. He tried to treat his daughter as he saw other fathers and mothers treat their children. He was anxious for her to be happy here in their new home, but it was his duty to teach her proper behavior and respect for adults. Among the Amish, a willful and disobedient child was proof of a neglectful father. It was the way he'd been taught and the way his parents had raised him.

The trouble was that Amelia didn't see things that way. She wasn't a sulky child, and her mind was sharp. Sometimes Caleb thought that she was far too clever to be four, almost five years of age. She could be affectionate toward him, but she seemed to take pleasure in doing exactly the opposite of what she was asked to do.

With a groan, Caleb raked his fingers through his hair. What was he going to do about Amelia? So far, his attempts at finding suitable childcare had fallen short. He'd hired two different girls, and both had walked out on him in less than three weeks' time.

Back in Idaho, his neighbor, widow Bea Mullet, had cared for Amelia when Caleb needed babysitting. She had come three days a week to clean the house, cook and tend to Amelia. But Bea was in her late seventies, not as spry as she had once been and her vision was poor. The truth was, Amelia had mostly run wild when he wasn't home to see to her himself. Once the bishop's wife had even spoken to him about the untidy condition of Amelia's hair and prayer bonnet, and another time the deacon had complained about the child giggling during service. He had felt that that criticism was unfair. Males and females sat on opposite sides of the room during worship and children, naturally, were under the watchful eyes of the women. How was he supposed to discipline his daughter from across the room without interrupting the sermon?

Amelia was young and spirited. She had no mother to teach her how she should behave. Those were the excuses he'd made for her, but this morning, the truth was all too evident. Amelia was out of control. So exasperated was he, that—had he been a father who believed in physical punishment—Amelia would have been soundly spanked. But he lacked the stomach to do it. No matter what, he could never strike a child.

Caleb shook his head. He'd ignored the good advice that friends and fellow church members had offered. He'd come to Delaware to put the past behind him, but he'd brought his own stubborn willfulness with him. He'd allowed a four-year-old child to run wild. And this disaster was the result.

"Good morning," came a cheerful female voice, startling Caleb.

He looked up and stared at the young woman standing just inside his kitchen. She'd come through the utility room.

"The door was open." She whipped off a navy blue wool scarf and he caught a glimpse of red-gold hair beneath her *kapp.* Sparkling drops of water glistened on her face.

Caleb opened his mouth to reply, but she was too quick for him.

"I'm Rebecca. Rebecca Yoder. We met on your barn beam the other night."

She offered a quick smile as she shed a dark rain slicker. Beneath it, she wore a lavender dress, a white apron and black rubber boots—two boots. Unlike him. Suddenly, Caleb was conscious of how foolish he must look, standing there with one bare foot, his hair uncombed and sticking up like a rooster's comb and his shirt-tails hanging out of his trousers.

"My door was open?" he repeated, woodenly.

Fritzy, the traitor, wagged his stump of a tail so hard that his whole backside wiggled back and forth. He sat where Caleb had commanded him to stay, but it was clear that given the choice he would have rushed up to give the visitor a hearty welcome kiss.

"*Ya.* I'm guessing you weren't the one who left it open." She pulled off first one rubber boot and then the other and hung the rain-streaked slicker on an iron hook. "I'm here to help with the housework. And Amelia."

She looked at him and then slowly scanned the room, taking in the spilled flour, the cluttered table and the floor. Her freckled nose wrinkled, and he was struck by how young and fetching she appeared. "Eli told you that I was coming, didn't he?"

Eli? Caleb's mind went blank. "*N...ne.* He didn't."

"Yesterday. He was supposed to tell you that I…" She shrugged. "Fannie sent me. Fannie Byler. She said you needed someone to…"

He couldn't remember Eli or anyone mentioning sending another girl. Certainly not the Yoder girl. "They sent you?"

Rebecca's small fists rested on her shapely hips. "You're not still angry about Friday night?" Her smile became a chuckle.

"I'm not angry," he protested. "But you're…you're too…too…" He was going to say *young,* but he knew she was at least twenty-one. Maybe twenty-two. Old enough to have her own child. "Inexperienced. Amelia is… Can be…difficult. She—" What he was trying to say was lost in the sound of Fritzy gagging. He groaned out loud. The ham Amelia had given him was far too rich for the dog's stomach. "Outside!" Caleb yelled. "If you're going to be sick, do it outside!" He pushed past Rebecca and dashed through the small utility room to throw open the back door.

Not quite in time.

Fritzy made it out of the kitchen but lost it on the cement floor in front of the washing machine. "Out!" Caleb repeated. Sheepishly, the dog bounded out into the yard, where he proceeded to run in circles and snap at the raindrops. Now that his stomach had yielded up the large plate of ham, Fritzy was obviously cured.

Caleb returned to the kitchen to deal with Rebecca Yoder. "You have to go," he said.

"Ne," she replied, smiling again. *"You* have to go. Roman and Eli will be waiting for you. There's a big truck there already. Eli said yesterday they were expecting your saws this morning."

"I don't need your help."

"You don't?" She slowly scanned the kitchen. "It looks to me as if that's exactly what you do need." She tapped her lips with a slender finger. "I know what the other girls said, about why they quit. I know what they said about Amelia and about you."

"About me?" The trouble was with his daughter. What fault could those young women have found in *his* behavior? He hadn't done or said anything—

"They said you are abrupt and hard to please." She sounded...amused.

"I am not!"

"Dat!"

Caleb turned toward the sound of Amelia's voice. She was standing in the kitchen doorway, still in her wet and muddy nightgown, her face streaked with tears. In one hand she held a pair of scissors, and in the other, a large section of her long, dark hair.

"Amelia?" He grabbed the scissors. "What have you done?"

"I'll tend to her," Rebecca assured him without the least bit of concern in her voice. She walked calmly over to Amelia, as if little girls cut their hair every day. "This is women's work. Isn't it, Amelia?" She looked down at the little girl.

Amelia looked up at her, obviously unsure what to think.

Caleb hesitated. He couldn't just walk out and leave his daughter with this girl, could he? What if that only made things worse?

"I'll be here just as a trial," Rebecca said. "A week. If we don't suit, then you can find someone else."

Caleb didn't know what to say. He really didn't have a choice, did he? The men would be waiting for him. "A week? *Ya.*" He nodded, on firmer ground again. He wouldn't be that far away. It might be easier to let this young woman try and fail than to argue with her. "Just a week," he repeated. He looked at Amelia. "Dat has to go to work," he said. "This... Rebecca will look after you…and help you tidy up your breakfast." He looked around the kitchen and shuddered inwardly. "I hope you are made of sterner stuff than the past two girls," he said to Rebecca.

"We'll see," Rebecca answered as she gathered the still-weeping child in her arms. "Breakfast and clean clothing for Amelia…and two boots for you are a start, wouldn't you agree?"

The strenuous task of unloading the heavy saws and woodworking equipment took all of Caleb's concentration for three hours. But when the truck pulled away and he was left alone to organize the tools in his area partitioned off in Roman's shop, his thoughts returned to Rebecca and his daughter. What if he'd been so eager to get out of the house and to his tools that he'd left Amelia with someone unsuited to the task? What if Amelia disliked Rebecca or was fearful of her? What if Amelia had been so bad that Rebecca had walked out and left the child alone?

Once doubt had crept into his mind, Caleb began to worry in earnest. The thing to do, he decided as he slid a chisel into place on a rack, would be to walk back home and check on them. It wasn't unreasonable that a father make certain that his new housekeeper was doing her job and watching over Amelia. It was still spitting rain, but what of it? And there was the matter of the blister on his heel, where his shoe had rubbed against his bare foot for the past few hours. Putting a Band-Aid on the blister made sense. He couldn't afford to be laid up with an infection, not with the important contract to fulfill in the next thirty-eight days.

Caleb surveyed his new workbench and tables. This

was a larger space than he'd had on his farm back in Idaho. Once everything was in place—drills, fretsaw, coping saws, hammers, mallets, sanders, planes, patterns and the big, gas-powered machinery—he could start work. Many of his tools were old, some handed down from his great-grandfather. The men in his family had always been craftsmen and had earned their living as cabinetmakers and builders of fine furniture. Only a few of his family's personal antiques had survived the fire: a walnut Dutch cupboard carved with the date 1704, a small cherry spice cabinet, and an *aus schteier kischt,* a blanket chest painted with unicorns, hearts and flowers that would one day be part of Amelia's bridal dowry.

A tickle at the back of Caleb's throat made him swallow. He didn't want to think of Amelia growing up and leaving him to be a wife. He knew it must be, but she was all he had and he wanted to keep her close by him for a long, long time. Impatient with his foolishness— worrying about her marriage when she had yet to learn her letters and still slept with her thumb in her mouth— he pushed away thoughts of Amelia as an adult. What should concern him was her safety right now. He'd abandoned her to the care of a girl barely out of her teens. For all he knew his daughter might be neglected. She could be sliding down the wet roof or swimming in the horse trough.

Slamming the pack of fine sandpaper down on the workbench, he turned and strode toward the door that led outside to the parking lot. He swung it open and nearly collided with Rebecca Yoder, who was just coming in. In her hands, she carried a Thermos, and just behind her was Amelia with his black lunchbox. They were both wearing rain slickers and boots. Caleb had no idea how they had found Amelia's rain slicker. It had been missing for days.

Caleb sputtered his apologies and stepped out of their way. He could feel his face flaming, and once again, he couldn't think of anything sensible to say to Rebecca. "I…I was on my way home," he managed. "To see about Amelia."

His daughter giggled. "I'm here, Dat. We brought your lunch." She held up the big black lunchbox.

"And hot cider." Rebecca raised the Thermos. "It's such a raw day, Amelia thought you'd like something hot."

"Not coffee," Amelia said. "I hate coffee. But…but I like cider."

"There's a table with benches in the next room," Rebecca suggested. "Eli and Roman eat lunch there when they don't go home. I know Eli's there." She pointed toward a louvered door on the far side of the room.

"I helped cook your lunch," his daughter proclaimed proudly. "I cooked the eggs. All by myself!"

"She did," Rebecca agreed. "And she filled a jar with coleslaw. There's some chicken corn soup and biscuits we made. But Amelia said you liked hard-boiled eggs."

"With salt and pepper." Amelia bounced up and down so hard that the lunchbox fell out of her hands.

Caleb stooped to pick it up.

"Ooh!" Amelia cried.

"It's all right," he assured her. "Nothing broken." He followed Rebecca and a chattering Amelia into the lunchroom. He didn't know what else to do. And as he did, he noticed that under her raincoat, Amelia looked surprisingly neat. Her face was so clean it was shiny and her hair was plaited into two tiny braids that peeked out from under an ironed *kapp*. Even the hem of her blue dress that showed under her slicker was pressed.

"What…what did you two do this morning?" he asked Amelia.

"We cleaned, Dat. And cooked. And I helped." She nodded. "I did."

No tears, no whining, no fussing. Amelia looked perfectly content.… More than content. He realized that she looked happy. He should have been pleased—he was pleased—but there was something unsettling about this young Yoder woman.

Rebecca stopped and glanced back over her shoulder at him. Her face was smooth and expressionless, but a dimple and the sparkle in her blue eyes made him suspect that she was finding this amusing. "Do you approve?"

"Wait until I see what my kitchen looks like," he answered gruffly.

Amelia giggled. "I told you, Dat. We cleaned."

Rebecca's right eyebrow raised and her lips quivered with suppressed laughter. "A week's trial," she reminded him. "That's all I agreed to. By then I should know if I want to work for you."

Chapter Four

On Friday, Caleb left work a half hour early and started home. He'd finished the ornate Victorian oak bracket that he'd been fashioning all afternoon, and he didn't want to begin a new piece so late in the day. Three years ago, he'd switched from building custom kitchen cabinets to the handcrafted corbels, finials and other architectural items that he sold to a restoration supply company in Boise. Englishers who fixed up old houses all over the country spent an exorbitant amount of money to replicate original wooden details. Not that Caleb wasn't glad for the business, but he guessed his thrifty Swiss ancestors would be shocked at the expense of fancy things when plain would do.

He rarely left his workbench before five, but he was still uneasy leaving Amelia with the Yoder girl. Better to arrive early and check up on them. So far, Rebecca Yoder seemed capable, and he had to admit that his daughter liked her, but time would tell. Amelia sometimes went days without getting into real mischief. And then, it was Gertie, bar the door—meaning that his sweet little girl could stir up some real trouble.

The walk home from the shop took only a few minutes, but his new workshop was far enough from his house to be respectable. Otherwise, it wouldn't have been fitting for him to have an unmarried girl housekeeping and watching his daughter for him. He left in the morning when Rebecca arrived and she went home in the late afternoon when he returned from work. The schedule was working out nicely, and as much as he hated to admit it, it was nice to know that someone would be there in the house when he arrived home. A house could get lonely with just a man and his little girl.

When Caleb arrived home, Rebecca's pony was pastured beside his driving horse, and the two-wheeled, open buggy that she'd ridden in this morning was waiting by the shed. A basket of green cooking apples, three small pumpkins and a woman's sewing box filled the storage space at the rear of the buggy. As he crossed the yard toward the house, Caleb noticed that one of the kitchen windows stood open. Wonderful smells drifted out, becoming stronger as he let himself in through the back door into an enclosed porch that served as a laundry and utility room.

Fritzy greeted him, stump of a tail wagging, and Caleb paused to scratch the dog behind his ears. "I'm home," he called. And then, to Fritzy, he murmured in *Deitsch,* "Good boy, good old Fritzy."

Amelia's delighted squeal rang out, and Caleb grinned, pleased that she was so happy to see him. But when he stepped into the kitchen, he discovered that his daughter's attention was riveted on an aluminum colander hanging on the back of a chair.

"Again!" Amelia cried. "Let me try again!"

"Ne," Rebecca said. "My turn now. You have to wait until it's your turn."

"One!" Amelia yelled.

Caleb watched, bewildered, as an object flew through the air to land in the colander.

"Two!" Into the colander.

"Three!"

A third one bounced off the back of the chair and slid across the floor to rest at his feet.

"You missed!" Amelia crowed. "My turn!"

"Vas ist das?" Caleb demanded, picking up what appeared to be a patchwork orange beanbag. "What's going on?"

"Dat!" Amelia whirled around, flung herself across the room and leaped into his arms. "We're playing a throwing game," she exclaimed, somehow extracting the cloth beanbag from his hand and nearly whacking him in the eye with it as she climbed up to lock her arms around his neck. "At Fifer's Orchard they had games and a straw maid and—"

"A maze," Rebecca corrected. "A straw bale maze."

"And a train," Amelia shouted. "A little one. For *kinder* to ride on. And a pumpkin patch. You get on a wagon and a tractor pulls you—"

Caleb's brow creased in a frown. "A train? You let Amelia ride on a toy train like the Englisher children?" His gaze fell on a large orange lollipop propped on the table. The candy was shaped like a pumpkin on a stick, wrapped in clear paper and tied with a ribbon. "And you bought her English sweets?" Caleb extricated himself from Amelia's stranglehold, unwound her arms and lowered her gently to the floor. "Do you think that was wise?" he asked, picking up the lollipop and turning it over to frown at the jack-o'-lantern face painted on the back. "These things are not for Amish children."

"*Ya,* so I explained to her and I'd explain to you if you'd let me speak," Rebecca said, a saucy tone to her voice. "We weren't the only Amish there. And it was Bishop Atlee's wife who bought the lollipop for her. I could hardly take it back and offend the woman. I told Amelia that she couldn't have it unless you approved, and then only after her supper. I didn't allow her to go into the Fall Festival area with the straw maze, the rides and the face painting. I told her that those things were fancy, not plain."

"But…" he began.

Rebecca went on talking. "Amelia didn't fuss when I told her no, and she helped me pick a basket of apples." Rebecca flashed him a smile. "Three of those apples are baking with brown sugar in the oven. For after your evening meal or tomorrow's breakfast."

Caleb ran a finger under his collar. He could feel heat creeping up his throat and his cheeks were suddenly warm. Once again this red-haired Yoder girl was making him feel foolish in his own house. "So she didn't ride the toy train?"

"A wagon, Dat." Amelia tossed the orange bean-bag into the air. "Rebecca said that we could…to pick pumpkins and apples."

"To find the best ones," Rebecca explained. "We had to go to the field, so we rode the tractor wagon. Otherwise we couldn't have carried it all back."

"Too heavy!" Amelia exclaimed, catching hold of his hand and tugging him toward the stove. "And we made a stew—in a pumpkin! For supper!" Amelia bounced and twirled, coming perilously near the stove. He caught her around the waist and scooped her up out of danger as she chattered on without a pause for breath. "I helped, Dat. Rebecca let me help."

Caleb exhaled, definitely feeling outnumbered and outmatched. The good smells, he realized, were coming from the oven. A cast-iron skillet of golden-brown biscuits rested on the stovetop beside a saucepan of what could only be fresh applesauce. "Maybe I was too hasty," he managed. "But the beanbags? The money I left in the sugar bowl was for groceries, not toys. The move from Idaho was expensive. I can't afford to buy—"

"I stitched up the beanbags at home last night."

Rebecca's expression was innocent, but she couldn't hide the light of amusement in her vivid blue eyes.

"From scraps," she continued. "And I stuffed them with horse corn. So they aren't really *bean*bags."

"Corn bags!" Amelia giggled. "You have to play, Dat. It's fun. You count, and you try to throw the bags into the coal-ander."

"Colander." Rebecca returned her attention to Caleb. "It's educational. To teach the little ones to count in English. Mam has the same game at the school. The children love it."

Caleb's mouth tightened, and he grunted a reluctant assent. "If the toy is made and not bought, I suppose—"

"You try, Dat," Amelia urged. "Rebecca can do it. It's really hard to get them in the coal…colander." She pushed an orange bag into his hand. "And you have to count," she added in *Deitsch*. "In English!"

"I don't have time to play with you now," Caleb hedged. "The rabbits need—"

"We fed the bunnies," Amelia said. "And gave them water."

"And fresh straw," Rebecca added. She moved to the stove and poured a mug of coffee. "But maybe you're tired after such a long day at the shop." She raised a russet eyebrow. "Sugar and cream?"

Caleb shook his head. "Black."

"My father always liked his coffee black, too," Rebecca murmured, "but I like mine with sugar and cream." She held out the coffee. "I just made it fresh."

"Please, Dat," Amelia begged, tugging on his arm. "Just one game."

His gaze met his daughter's, and his resolve to have none of this silliness melted. Such a little thing to bring a smile to her face, he rationalized...and he had been away from her all day. "Three throws," he agreed, "but then—"

"Yay!" Amelia cried. "Dat's going to try."

"You have to stand back by the window," Rebecca instructed. "Underhand works better."

With a sigh, Caleb took to the starting point and tossed all three beanbags into the colander on the first try, one after another.

"*Gut,* Dat!" Amelia hopped from one foot to the other, wriggling with joy. "But you forgot to count. Now my turn. You take turns." She gathered up the beanbags and moved back about three feet. "One...*zwei*...three!" She burst into giggles as she successfully got one of the three into the target.

"A tie," Rebecca proclaimed, and when he looked at her in surprise, she said, "Amelia gets a handicap." She shrugged and gave a wry smile. "Both on the English and on her aim." Rebecca stepped to a spot near the utility room door, a little farther from the colander than he stood, and lobbed all of the bags in. She didn't forget to count in English.

"Rebecca wins!" Amelia declared. "She beat you, Dat. You forgot to count."

Caleb grimaced. "I did, didn't I?"

Rebecca nodded. "You did."

"The lamb's tail," Amelia supplied and giggled again.

"Comes last," Rebecca finished for her.

He chuckled and took a sip of his coffee. It was good and strong, the way he liked it. But there was something extra. He sniffed the mug. Had Rebecca added something? "Vanilla?" he asked.

"Just a smidgen," Rebecca admitted. "My father liked his that way."

Caleb nodded and took another sip. "Not bad," he pronounced, and then said, "Since I'm new at this corn-bag tossing, I think I deserve a rematch."

"The champion sits out," Rebecca explained merrily. "So you have to play Amelia."

Caleb groaned. "Why do I think that there's no way I can win this?"

"I go first," Amelia said, scooping up the bag. *"Eins."* She tossed the first.

"One," Caleb corrected. "You have to say it in English, remember?"

"Two! *Drei!*" she squealed, throwing the third.

"Three," he said. "One, two, three."

"I got them all in," Amelia said. "All *drei.*"

"She did," Rebecca said. "All *three* in. That will be hard to beat, Caleb."

He pretended to be worried, making a show of staring at the colander and pacing off the distance backward. Amelia giggled. "Shh," he said. "I'm concentrating here." When he got back to his spot by the window, he spun around, turning his back to them and tossed the first beanbag over his shoulder. It fell short, and Amelia clapped her hands and laughed.

"You forgot to count again," she reminded him.

Caleb clapped one hand to his cheeks in mock dismay. "Can I try again?"

"Two more," Amelia agreed, "and then it's my turn again."

He spun back around and closed his eyes. "Two!" he declared and let it fly.

There was a *plop* and a shocked gasp. When Caleb opened his eyes, it was to see Martha Coblentz—the other preacher's wife—standing in the doorway that opened to the utility room, her hands full, her mouth opening and closing like a beached fish.

Well, it should be, Caleb thought as familiar heat washed over his neck and face. The beanbag had landed on Martha's head and appeared to be lodged in her prayer *kapp*. The shame he felt at being caught in the midst of such childish play was almost as great as his overwhelming urge to laugh. "I'm sorry," he exclaimed, covering his amusement with a choking cough. "It was a game. My daughter… We… I was teaching her English…counting…"

Martha drew herself to her full height and puffed up like a hen fluffing her feathers. The beanbag dislodged, bounced off her nose and landed on the floor. "Well, I never!" she said as her gaze raked the kitchen, taking in Rebecca, the colander, the biscuits on the stove and the pumpkin lollipop on the table. Martha sniffed and sent the beanbag scooting across the clean kitchen floor with the toe of one sensible, black-leather shoe. "Hardly what I expected to find here." Her lips pursed into a thin, lard-colored line. "Thought you'd want something hot…for your supper."

Caleb realized that Martha wasn't alone. A younger woman—Martha and Reuben's daughter, Doris, Dorothy, something like that—stood behind her, her arms full of covered dishes. She shifted from side to side, craning her thin neck to see past her mother.

"Come in," Caleb said. "Please. Have coffee."

"Aunt Martha. Dorcas." Rebecca, not seeming to be the least bit unsettled by their arrival, smiled warmly and motioned to them. "I know you have time for coffee."

"Your mother said you were only here while Preacher Caleb was at the shop," Martha said. "I didn't expect to find such goings-on."

"We came to bring you stuffed beef heart." Dorcas offered him a huge smile. One of her front teeth was missing, making the tall, thin girl even plainer. "And liver dumplings." The young woman had a slight lisp.

Caleb hated liver only a little less than beef heart. He swallowed the lump in his throat and silently chided himself for being so uncharitable to two of his flock, especially Dorcas, so obedient and modestly dressed. He had a long way to go to live up to his new position as preacher for this congregation.

"And molasses shoofly pie," Martha added proudly, holding it up for his approval. "Dorcas made it herself, just for you." She strode to the table, set down the dessert and picked up the questionable pumpkin lollipop by the end of the ribbon. Holding it out with as much disgust as she might have displayed for a dead mouse attached to a trap, Martha carried the candy to the trash can and dropped it in. "Surely, you weren't going to allow your child to eat such English junk," she said, fixing him with a reproving stare. "Our bishop would never approve of jack-o'-lantern candy, but of course, I'd never mention it to him."

"Pumpkin," Rebecca said, defending the lollipop. "We were going to wash off the face."

Martha sniffed again, clearly not mollified.

Amelia's lower lip quivered. She cast one hopeful glance in Caleb's direction, and when he gave her the father warning look, she turned and pounded out of the room and up the stairs. Fritzy—cowardly dog that he was—fled, hot on the child's heels.

Rebecca went to the stove and turned off the oven. "You're right, Aunt Martha," she said sweetly. "It *is* time I went home."

Martha scowled at her.

"Eight on Monday?" Rebecca asked Caleb.

"Eight-thirty," he answered.

Rebecca collected the colander and the beanbags, made her farewells to her aunt and cousin and vanished into the utility room. "See you Sunday for church."

Martha bustled to the stove, shoved Rebecca's pan of biscuits aside and reached for one of the containers Dorcas carried. "Put the dumplings there." She indicated the countertop. "They're still warm," Martha explained. "But they taste just as good cold."

Probably not, Caleb thought, trying not to cringe. He liked dumplings well enough, although the ones the women cooked here in Delaware—slippery dumplings—were different than the ones he'd been served in Idaho. He certainly couldn't let good food go to waste, but he wasn't looking forward to getting Amelia to eat anything new. The beef heart would certainly be a challenge. His daughter could be fussy about her meals. Once she'd gone for two weeks on nothing but milk and bread and butter. That was her "white" phase, he supposed. And the butter only passed the test because it was winter and the butter was pale.

"We wondered how you were settling in," Martha said. "Such a pity, losing your wife the way you did. Preachers are generally married. I've never heard of one chosen who was a single man, but the Lord works in mysterious ways. He has His plan for us, and all we can do is follow it."

"Ya," Caleb agreed. The smell of the beef heart was strong, but fortunately not strong enough to cover the scent of Rebecca's stew baked in a pumpkin or the apples and cinnamon.

Martha eyed the biscuits. "I suppose you can eat those with your supper," she said. "Although my sister-by-marriage—Hannah Yoder, my dead brother's wife— has taught her girls to cook the Mennonite way. Hannah was born and raised Mennonite, not Amish," she said, wanting to make certain that he got her point. "Most prefer my recipe for baking powder biscuits. My Grossmama Yoder's way. She always used lard. Hannah uses butter." Martha curled her upper lip. "Too rich, by my way of thinking. Not plain."

"Ne," Dorcas agreed. "Mam's biscuits are better."

"But you'll love Dorcas's shoofly pie," Martha said, patting her daughter on the shoulder. "Extra molasses and a good crumb crust. That's the secret."

"Ya," Dorcas echoed. "That's the secret."

Caleb struggled to find something to say. Was he

supposed to invite them to stay for supper? It was early yet, but he was hungry—hungrier than he could remember being in a long time. There was something about this mild Delaware autumn that put a spring into his step and made his appetite hearty. "I thank you for your kindness, Martha. And you, Dorcas. I'm not much of a cook myself."

"Just so," Martha agreed. "And why would you be? Cooking is a woman's gift. Men's work and women's are separate." Something that might have been a smile creased the lower half of her face. "We'll be by again on Sunday with something else. Can't let our new preacher starve, can we, Dorcas?"

"Ne." Dorcas blushed and averted her gaze. "Can't let him starve."

Martha started for the door and Dorcas followed. "We'll get the china on Sunday," the older woman said. She spared a glance at the trash can. "And, mind you, no more of those pagan sweets for Amelia. Our bishop is strict. I can't imagine what his wife would say if she knew that Rebecca Yoder gave such nonsense to your innocent daughter."

Chapter Five

Two weeks later, on the last Sunday in October, church was held at Samuel and Anna's home, and the community got to hear the new preacher's first sermon. Caleb had chosen to speak on Moses and how—with the Lord's help—he led the Israelites out of slavery in Egypt, through the wastelands in search of the Promised Land. Prayers and scripture readings by Rebecca's Uncle Reuben aided Caleb; the main sermon on faith and patience in the face of impossible odds was delivered by Bishop Atlee. Everyone had an opinion about Caleb's sermon, but most agreed that it was a good one for a beginner.

"Plainspoken is what I say," Lydia Beachy declared later as she collected dirty plates from the long table in the backyard and placed them in a tub of soapy water. The deep container fitted neatly in the back of a child's wagon pulled by Rebecca. Men, women and children had all finished eating, and the women and girls were busy cleaning up before a short prayer session that would end the day's worship. "The man is plainspoken."

"But that's a good thing in a preacher." Martha

picked up a handful of dirty silverware, glanced across the yard toward the group of men lounging against the barn and lowered her voice. "My Reuben has a real gift for delivering a sermon, but he can let the time get away from him."

Rebecca averted her eyes and pressed her lips tightly together to keep from smiling. Uncle Reuben was known for his long sermons, preaching sessions that Bishop Atlee sometimes tactfully cut short by asking that the congregation rise for a hymn from the *Ausbund*. But Uncle Reuben had been chosen to minister to the flock, and such thoughts, she decided, were uncharitable—especially on a church Sunday.

Lydia nodded to give emphasis to her statements. She was tall and thin, and her head bobbing was so vigorous when she spoke that Rebecca always expected her *kapp* to fly off like a startled pigeon.

"No one could call Caleb long-winded," Lydia declared in her always-squeaky voice. "In my opinion, he might have been a bit nervous, but who wouldn't be his first time preaching?" She folded her arms and looked right into Aunt Martha's face. "Can you imagine standing up there and having to give a sermon?"

"Ne." Aunt Martha's mouth and eyes opened wide. "Wherever do you get those ideas, Lydia Beachy?" She scoffed. "A woman preaching a sermon? *Narrisch!*" *Crazy.*

And it was a strange idea, Rebecca had to agree. A baptized woman's vote was equal to a man's in the church, but women couldn't be preachers or bishops. And Rebecca wouldn't want to be. She'd been so nervous that when Caleb first stood up, his face pale, his hands clamped tight against his sides, she'd held her breath. But as he'd begun to talk, he'd looked out at his neighbors and began to speak naturally. He had a clear, strong voice, and a way of speaking that painted pictures of that long-ago time in her mind. If she closed her eyes, she could still see the Israelites, with all their children and their flocks, fleeing the Egyptian pharaoh's army. And she could almost hear the crash of waves as the sea closed around the soldiers and washed them away.

Aunt Martha said Caleb's sermon had lasted the better part of an hour, but for Rebecca the time had flown by. She felt that he deserved the praise that people were giving him.

"A blessing for us that the day remained so mild," her mother Hannah said as she whisked a food-stained tablecloth off the bare table, rolled it up and handed it to Rebecca's friend, Mary Byler. The table, really a series of folding tables, stretched more than thirty feet and required six tablecloths to cover it. Tomorrow, Anna would wash the linens and hang them out on the line to dry, but not today. No work, other than caring for livestock or what must be done for the family, was allowed on Sunday.

The day had been unseasonably warm, and much to everyone's delight, the church members had been able to share their communal meal outside in the yard—probably for the last Sunday of the autumn. Rebecca always loved eating outside at church. It made the afternoon almost a holiday.

Mam nudged Rebecca's elbow and motioned toward the back porch. Anna's daughter Mae, Amelia and two other little girls were gathered around Susanna, listening as she "read" a Bible story. Of course, Susanna couldn't really read all the words in the book, but she knew them by heart and could recite them well enough to satisfy the children. Vigorous play wasn't encouraged on the Sabbath, and it was sometimes difficult to keep active little ones suitably occupied.

"Amelia's been a good girl today." Hannah smiled. "You've done wonders with her."

Rebecca nodded. "I only had to take her out of service twice, once to use the bathroom and later when she was getting hungry. And so far, no temper tantrums."

"Just wait," Mary said. "That Amelia's a handful. Just when you think she's behaving and being nice... *Wham.* A dead mouse in your apron pocket." She rolled her eyes. "And the apple doesn't fall far from the tree. If you ask me, I'd say our new preacher has a sharp side, as well."

"I haven't seen it since I've been working there," Rebecca said. She felt that her friend had gone overboard in finding fault with the little girl and, for that matter, with her father. Other than a few setbacks, she'd made out fine at Caleb's house, and she had to admit, she looked forward to going every day. "Amelia's like any four-year-old," Rebecca defended. "She gets into mischief sometimes, but she's sweet natured."

"Sweet like honeycomb in the hive," Mary murmured, half under her breath. "Full of bee stings." Rebecca's mother handed Mary another soiled tablecloth, and Mary bundled an armload together. "I'll take these to the washroom and come back for the others."

"I'll get the rest," Lydia offered. "You can put the rest of those sandwiches in the refrigerator with the macaroni salad and wipe down the counters."

While work wasn't permitted on Sundays, necessary work like cleaning up dirty dishes and putting food away was.

"Services will be starting soon," Rebecca said.

"But you can't leave those hard-boiled eggs out." Aunt Martha pointed to a bowl. "It's too warm in the kitchen."

"We won't," Mary assured her as she started back toward the house with the armload of tablecloths.

Mam and Lydia exchanged looks. "I'm sorry that Mary had a difficult time with Caleb's daughter," Mam said, folding her arms. "But Rebecca hasn't come home with any complaints."

Lydia shrugged. "*Kinner* can be a handful. Especially at that age. I'll give credit where credit is due," she continued. "Rebecca, you've done well with that family." A smiled creased her thin face, making her look younger than her mid-forties. "From what Fannie told me…"

Roman's wife, round and rosy-cheeked Fannie, her hands full with a dishpan of coffee mugs, bustled toward them. "What did Fannie say?" she asked Lydia good-naturedly.

Mam and Lydia chuckled.

Rebecca liked both Fannie and Lydia. They were close friends of her mother's, and Rebecca had known them since she was a baby. They seemed more like relatives than neighbors. Although Fannie and Lydia loved gossip as well as most, there wasn't a mean bone in either one's body. And if someone needed help, Amish or English, Fannie and Lydia were likely to trample each other trying to get there to give assistance.

"Didn't I tell you Fannie had good hearing? You can't get anything past her," Hannah teased.

"I was only saying what you told me before services,

Fannie," Lydia said. "That you were in Caleb Wittner's house on and off while Mary and then Lilly worked for him. You said that things were different since Hannah's Rebecca took over. You said that Rebecca had put that place in order. And the child is better behaved."

"*Ya,* I did say so, Hannah." Fannie nodded. "Not to be speaking ill of Caleb or of little Amelia. Wouldn't do that. Eli's cousin is a good man and a hard worker. It can't be easy for him to tend a house and care for a motherless girl. Poor man, he means well, but he just never seemed to have his household in order. Our Rebecca's made a world of difference."

"You shouldn't be saying such things. You'll puff her up with false pride," Aunt Martha warned. Fannie shrugged. "Truth is truth, Martha. Mary and Lilly together couldn't do what Rebecca has done for Caleb's family."

Rebecca felt her cheeks grow warm. It was good to hear that Fannie approved of what she'd done with Amelia, but Mary and Lilly were her friends. It wasn't right to make light of their efforts. "*Ya,* Caleb's house did need readying up," she admitted. "But he'd just moved in when Mary and Lilly helped out. Just coming from Idaho to Delaware had to be upsetting to Amelia." Feeling uncomfortable, Rebecca glanced across to where the men stood and was surprised to find Caleb watching her.

"If Rebecca has such a touch with that girl, she'd better see to her," Martha retorted, pointing. "Looks to me as though the pot has just boiled over."

Rebecca turned in time to see Amelia, on the porch, give Mae a hard shove that sent her tumbling off the back step. Susanna protested and Amelia answered back. Then Mae began to wail and Amelia burst into tears.

Rebecca grimaced.

"Go on," Mam said. "Straighten it out."

By the time Rebecca reached the porch, Amelia had worked herself up into a full-blown fuss.

Susanna was attempting to quiet her, to no avail. "She hit Mae and pushed her off the step," Susanna said. "And…and Mae hurt her knee."

Mae's black cotton stocking was torn, and Rebecca saw a small scrape and a few drops of blood. Mae, naturally, was making the most of the incident, howling like a hound dog on the trail of a rabbit. "She hurt me," Mae blubbered.

"I hate her!" Amelia shouted between outbursts of angry tears.

Rebecca gathered her charge—kicking and screaming—and whisked her into the house. As she carried the child through the back doorway and into the kitchen crowded with women and babies, she ignored unrequested advice sent in her direction and hurried through the kitchen and the rows of benches set up in the living room for church services. She turned into a wide hallway and found the spacious downstairs bathroom. Rebecca closed and locked the door behind them, and deposited the still-hysterical Amelia on the floor.

The girl stomped her foot and swung a fist at her. "I hate you, too!"

"Shh, shh, sweetie, you don't hate anyone," Rebecca soothed. She knelt on the floor so that she was eye to eye with the frustrated child. "Now, tell me what's wrong."

Amelia's features crumpled and she began to cry in

earnest. Rebecca held out her arms and the little girl first hesitated, then ran into them. "Mae said…said…I don't have a mother," she sobbed. "An…and I do so." Her thin shoulders trembled. "I do."

"Of course you do," Rebecca answered. "She's still your mother, even if she can't be here with you."

Amelia drew in a long, ragged sob. "Mae said…said she has a mother and I don't."

"Shh, shh," Rebecca soothed, cradling the child against her. "That wasn't very nice of Mae."

"She said…" Amelia pulled away and rubbed her eyes with her fists. "She said my Mam went to heaven because I was bad."

"Ne." Rebecca shook her head. "It was an accident. If you ask your *dat,* he'll explain it to you."

"Mae is mean. She wouldn't let me look at the book with the giraffe. She said she can read and I can't."

"I'll tell you a secret, Amelia. Mae was pretending. She can't read yet, either. But when you are a little older, you'll go to school and then you'll both learn."

"I hate her."

Rebecca sighed. "You don't hate her. Mae is your friend. She let you play with her Noah's ark, remember? Sometimes friends say unkind things to each other, but it doesn't mean that you stop liking each other."

Amelia sniffed. "I wasn't going to take her book home. I just wanted to look at the pictures."

"She should have shared with you." Rebecca gave Amelia another hug. "Let me wash your face."

"My tummy hurts."

"I know, but you'll feel better with a clean face." Rebecca stood up, ran cool water on a clean washcloth and wiped the tears and sweat from Amelia's face. "You know, Mae's first mother, the one whose tummy she grew in, died, too. She's in heaven with your *mam*. My sister Anna is Mae's new mother. So, for a long time, Mae was just like you."

Amelia's eyes widened. "She was? Did her *mam* die in a fire?"

Rebecca flinched. She hadn't known that Amelia was aware of the details of her mother's passing. Compassion made Rebecca's eyes blur with unshed tears. "*Ne,* sweet. Mae's *mam* was very sick and she couldn't get better."

"Will my *dat* get sick like that?"

Rebecca shook her head. "He is a big, strong man, Amelia. Nothing bad will happen to him." She wondered if it was wrong to say such a thing to an innocent child. Especially when her own father had been taken far too young. But she didn't have the heart to say otherwise. "You must trust in God, Amelia. Say your prayers and try to do what is right. And you mustn't hit or push or get angry with your friends."

"She was mean." Amelia pushed out her lower lip stubbornly. "She wouldn't let me share her book."

"That was wrong," Rebecca agreed, "but hitting and pushing were *two* wrongs. You'll have to think about that."

"And say I'm sorry?"

"Only if you really are," Rebecca pronounced. "Not if you don't want to."

Amelia chewed at the protruding lip. "Will I get a new mother, too?"

"Maybe," Rebecca said. "*Ya,* I think maybe you will."

"When?"

Rebecca shook her head. "Only God and your father know. And maybe your *dat* doesn't know, either. But someday, I'm sure you will."

"Will she be nice?"

"Absolutely. As nice as Anna is to Mae. And she will love you and take care of you."

"Like Mae?"

"*Ya,* just like Mae."

A sharp rapping on the bathroom door made the two of them jump.

"Amelia? Rebecca?" Caleb's voice.

"Yes?" Rebecca swallowed to dissolve the lump in her throat. Caleb sounded cross. Had he seen what happened with the children? "I was just—"

"Open the door."

Rebecca did as he asked. "Amelia's fine. She and Mae just had a little fuss and—"

"Amelia? Did Rebecca spank you?"

The little girl looked at her father and burst into tears. Rebecca blanched. "Spank her? *Ne,* I just—"

"I thought you said she was fine," Caleb said. "Look at her." Amelia flung herself into her father's embrace and started sobbing again.

"She *was* fine until you…" Rebecca tried to maintain her composure. "It was just a children's spat."

"If there was a problem, you should have called me. I'm her father. It isn't your place to discipline my child."

Amelia's wails became a shriek.

"I didn't *discipline* her." Against her will, Rebecca's eyes teared up. Caleb wasn't listening to her. He was judging her without hearing her side. "I was just trying to—"

"Your aunt told me what you were doing." He glared at her, his face contorted with anger.

"I don't care what anyone said. I would never—"

"When I need your help, I'll ask for it," Caleb said. Then he lifted Amelia into his arms and carried her out of the bathroom and down the hall.

Rebecca walked out of the bathroom, then turned, but not toward the parlor and living room where church members were already beginning to file in for the afternoon worship service. She went in the opposite direction.

She heard footsteps behind her and stopped, expecting to confront Caleb again. Instead she found that it was Mary.

"What happened?" Mary asked. "He yelled at you, didn't he? I heard him from the kitchen. What did he say?"

Rebecca shook her head. Mary was her friend, but she wasn't about to escalate the embarrassing situation. Bad enough that Caleb had been misinformed and believed it—believed that Rebecca would spank his child. She didn't want to distract the community from Sunday services and cause a bigger scene. "It doesn't matter what he said," Rebecca hedged. "Amelia was crying and Caleb thought I'd taken her into the bathroom to punish her."

"You wouldn't listen to me about him, would you?" Mary whispered with a satisfied expression. "But I told you so."

Chapter Six

The following morning, Rebecca arrived early at Caleb's house, not certain if she wanted to continue working for him—or if he wanted her. She'd gone over and over in her head what had happened the previous day, and she'd come to the conclusion that maybe she had overstepped her bounds in dealing with the incident between Mae and Amelia. As unusual as it was for a father to become involved in such a small matter in public, Caleb was Amelia's parent, her only parent. And if he believed that she'd overstepped her boundaries and interfered, he'd been right to be irritated with her.

Obviously, Aunt Martha had said something to Caleb that had agitated the situation. What she'd said Rebecca didn't know, but she could imagine. "Spare the rod and spoil the child." Aunt Martha loved to quote that, although Rebecca had never seen her aunt physically correct Dorcas or any other child. Rebecca had to believe that Aunt Martha hadn't meant to cause discord. Mam said Aunt Martha had a good heart under all her bluster; she just said whatever popped into her head without considering the harm it could do. Rebecca liked to think that Mam was right, but sometimes…sometimes it was difficult not to believe that her aunt enjoyed making mischief—especially for her sister-in-law Hannah and her daughters.

When Rebecca arrived at the farm, she found Caleb in the kitchen attempting to pack his lunch. Amelia, still in her nightgown and barefooted, was standing beside him, chattering away about Mae's giraffe book. When Rebecca entered the room, the little girl gave her a shy smile and ran to greet her.

"I'm hungry, Becca. Can I have pancakes for breakfast? I like pancakes. Blueberry. Can I?"

Rebecca removed her bonnet and hung it on a hook near the door, then added her cloak. It was cool this morning and the snap of autumn filled the air with the scents of wood smoke, newly split kindling and falling crimson and gold leaves. "Good morning, Caleb," she said hesitantly.

Fritzy gave a happy yelp and wagged his tail before dropping into a sitting position and raising one front paw.

"Good morning, Fritzy," Rebecca said. "Good boy."

Ignoring the dog, Caleb's eyes locked with Rebecca's, his steely gray gaze clouded with emotion. "I'm glad you came this morning." He looked at the floor, then back up at her. "I talked to Amelia. She told me what happened with Mae and what you said to her in the bathroom. I was wrong to jump to conclusions." Tiny wrinkles creased his forehead. "I owe you an apology." He swallowed. "I let my temper get the best of me, and I made a fool of myself. I hope you can forgive me."

"Ya," Rebecca murmured. "You did. Embarrass me,"

she added quickly. "I didn't mean to imply you were a fool."

"Only right if you did," he answered. He spread his hands, palm up, and Rebecca noticed a smear of mustard on his fingers. "I'm a blunt man. It's a fault of mine, and I fear I'm too old to overcome it. But I wronged you, and I intend to say so—not just to you, but to the community. Someone said something that made me think—"

"Aunt Martha," she supplied, going to the sink and retrieving a clean washcloth.

He nodded.

"Your hand," she said, running water on the cloth. She held it out to him. "Mustard…from your sandwich."

Caleb took the offered washcloth and cleaned off the mustard. "I'm all thumbs in the kitchen. Always was." He indicated the lumpy sandwich with bits of cheese and roughly cut ham spilling from the sides of the bread slices. Neither of them mentioned the obvious. His scarred hand didn't work as smoothly as the other. Not that he was handicapped. He managed his woodworking business, but using the burned hand was more awkward. "I'm apparently not much better in the role of preacher," he added.

Rebecca smiled gently. "I thought your sermon yesterday was a good one." A basket of clean laundry stood on the counter and Rebecca rifled through pillowcases and towels in search of socks for Amelia.

"Your opinion or that of the other members?"

"I only know what some of the women say. Mam gave you a B plus." Rebecca had worn a lavender dress today with the usual white apron. The garment was new. She'd finished stitching it on Mam's treadle machine on Saturday. It was as plain as her other dresses, but the cotton was soft and it was just the right weight for a fall day.

Caleb chuckled. "Bishop Atlee said I was a little long on the flight from Pharaoh's army and a little short on scripture." Caleb grimaced. "Too short altogether. He said that it was a good thing that Preacher Reuben can always be counted on to bring an abundance of sermon."

Caleb wore navy trousers, a light blue short-sleeved shirt and navy suspenders over his high-top, leather work shoes. It was what he wore every day but Sundays. Rebecca noticed that, as usual, his shirt was wrinkled. This one was also marred at the shoulder by what looked like a burn mark in the shape of an iron. She washed and ironed Amelia's clothes, but not Caleb's. He'd said that it wasn't fitting, and he liked to do his own laundry. Rebecca thought that he needed, at the very least, either help or instruction in the art of ironing.

Looking at his shirt, she thought how strange it was that she noticed the burn on his shirt first, not the scars on his face. His scars had been a little frightening the first time she'd seen them, but now she accepted them as part of Caleb. She simply didn't notice them when she looked at him. One side of his face, one hand, were smooth, and it was easy to imagine the other half as a mirror image...the way he'd been before the tragic fire.

She met his gaze. "I liked the part where you spoke about Moses's doubts when the Israelites were crossing the Red Sea and the soldiers were right behind them. That was good."

"I think I can understand a little of how he felt. Moses. God had called him, but he didn't feel up to the task." He opened a plastic bag and began to gather up his sandwich to put it in. "It's all new to me, preaching. I can't help thinking there are other men in the church who would do a better job."

"I can help," Amelia said.

"Wait—" Rebecca put out her hand to take Amelia's, but it was too late. Amelia pulled her father's sandwich to the edge of the counter, knocking half onto the floor. Fritzy dove for the bread and meat and gobbled it up.

"Fritzy!" Caleb said. The dog trotted to the far side of the kitchen, lay down and licked the crumbs off his chin with a long, red tongue.

"Not much left of your ham sandwich, I'm afraid," Rebecca said. "Do you like tuna salad?"

Caleb's mouth twisted into a grimace. "Like it fine. Don't have a can of tuna in the house. It doesn't matter. I can do without—"

"You can't work without your midday meal. Take this." She went to where she'd hung her cape and removed a foil-wrapped package from the pocket. "Two tuna sandwiches on rye with lettuce and mayonnaise. Mam was pushing them this morning. We had a lot of tuna salad left over from yesterday."

Caleb's face reddened. "I can't take your lunch."

"Of course you can. I'll just make some macaroni and cheese at nooning. Amelia loves mac and cheese." She looked at the little girl. "Don't you, Amelia?"

"Ya," the child agreed.

Caleb hesitated. "If you're sure…"

"I'm sure. I like mac and cheese, too, and we had tuna sandwiches for supper last night."

"All right." Caleb reached for the foil-wrapped sandwiches. "Thank you."

"You're welcome." Rebecca lifted Amelia onto a

chair and knelt to slip stockings on to her bare feet. "You need to find your shoes," she said. "The floor is cold." She glanced back at Caleb as Amelia jumped down off the chair. "What you said about you being a preacher. Grossmama says that God doesn't make mistakes. If He chose you for the job of preacher, it was the right decision."

"That's what I keep telling myself." He grabbed an apple off the counter and put it in a battered old black lunchbox, along with Rebecca's tuna sandwiches. "I may be a little late this afternoon. I have to finish cutting out some delicate pieces and pack them for a UPS pick up." In the doorway, he grabbed his straw hat and pulled it down over his forehead. He turned back to her. "I hope you'll accept my apology."

Rebecca looked at Caleb. "You've already apologized to me. There's no need to say anything more to me or to anyone else." *That would give people more to talk about,* she thought, but wisely didn't add.

"There's every need," he said gruffly as he reached for his denim jacket. "How can I point out the mistakes others make if I'm not willing to take responsibility for my own?"

"Is that how you think of it?" she asked. "A preacher's job is to point out mistakes?"

"Isn't it?"

She nibbled at her lower lip. "I think it's about being a shepherd, helping the flock to find water and a safe place to rest."

He shook his head. "People aren't sheep. I'm responsible for their souls."

She wasn't certain that she agreed his job was to point out the errors of people's ways, but it wasn't her place to argue. "I still don't think you need to say anything to anyone about what happened. It was such a small misunderstanding, Caleb. And I was partly in the wrong, too. I'm not Amelia's mother."

"*Ne.* You're not."

His face hardened and Rebecca wished she'd had the good sense to keep her mouth shut while she was ahead.

"Other than that, you're satisfied with my housekeeping and looking after Amelia?" she asked.

He shrugged. "Let's give each other a little more time." He patted Amelia on the head. "Be a good girl for Rebecca, pumpkin."

"Dat!" She giggled so hard that her nose wrinkled. "I'm not a pumpkin. I'm a girl."

"And a good thing, too, or Rebecca might be baking you into a pie." He tickled her belly.

And with that, Caleb was out of the house, leaving Rebecca confused and frustrated. What had just happened? He'd been so warm and friendly with her that she'd thought that everything was all right between them. And then he'd turned cold on her again.

She didn't know what to think, and she wished that she could talk the problem over with her mother or one of her sisters. One of the best things about having such a large family was that there was always someone to listen to you and share both good times and bad. But where Caleb was concerned, it didn't feel right. She was oddly reluctant to bring someone else, even someone she loved and trusted, into her confidence. Whether she kept the job or not, it was up to her to mend the breach with Caleb. The question was, how was she to do it?

"Rebecca. I'm hungry. I want pancakes."

"All right, pancakes it is," she agreed. "But we have no blueberries. I can make apple and cinnamon, if you like."

"Ya!" Amelia clapped her hands. "Apple."

Rebecca smiled to herself as she pulled out a mixing bowl, spoon, measuring cups and ingredients. Everyone in the community thought that Amelia was a problem child, but Rebecca felt that the problem lay with her father, the troublesome new preacher.

The week passed quietly for Caleb. When he'd met on Friday evening with Bishop Atlee, Deacon Samuel Mast and Reuben, he'd told them, "On Sunday, I raised my voice in anger to a young woman who'd done nothing wrong. I know that some of the congregation couldn't help but hear my foolish outburst. I think you should consider if my lapse in judgment is reason to dismiss me from my position as preacher."

For a moment, there'd been silence, and then Samuel laughed. "We're all as human as you," he had admitted. "And as likely to wade into muddy water when it comes to children's quarrels."

"Best to leave such matters to the women," Bishop Atlee had said.

"But as Amelia's father, isn't the responsibility mine?"

The bishop had stroked his gray beard thoughtfully. "And a heavy burden it must be for a man alone."

"Which is why you should find a wife," Reuben had advised.

"The sooner, the better." Samuel had leaned forward, elbows on the table. "I was widowed and left with young children, too, and the Lord led me to a good woman.

The only regret that I have is that I didn't ask her to marry me sooner."

Samuel's words echoed in Caleb's head now, as he rode in his buggy to Hannah Yoder's farm. Rebecca had invited Amelia to have supper with her family and had taken her home with her in the afternoon. It worked out for the best because Caleb had been unsure how long it would take to go over the church business, and he didn't want Rebecca to be out late. It would be simpler to carry a sleeping child home in his buggy than to worry about getting Rebecca home safely.

She met him at the back door and urged him to come in. "We have fresh coffee and apple-cranberry pie," she said.

"I thought I'd just pick up Amelia and—"

"Don't tell me that you don't have time for a slice of pie." Rebecca rested one hand on her hip.

He was about to refuse when his stomach betrayed him by rumbling. Pie was his weakness, and he hadn't had time to make himself anything substantial for supper before the meeting.

Stepping into the kitchen, he glanced around for Amelia. He didn't see her, but his gaze fell on the pie. The crust was brown and flaky, and it was impossible to draw a breath without inhaling the wonderful scents of apple, nutmeg and cinnamon.

"Irwin churned ice cream tonight for the children. There's plenty left." Rebecca motioned toward the table, poured him a mug of coffee and began cutting the pie. "Ice cream on top?"

Caleb groaned an assent, and in what seemed like seconds, he'd shrugged out of his jacket and a large slice of pie covered in a mound of vanilla ice cream had appeared in front of him.

Rebecca picked up a ball of yarn and two knitting needles and settled into a rocking chair near the window. She didn't speak, and the only sounds in the kitchen were the warm crackle from the woodstove, the tick of a mantel clock and the click of her needles. She didn't launch into chatter as she usually did mornings and evenings at his house, but only rocked and concentrated on the scarf she was constructing.

The chair Caleb sat in at the head of the table was big and comfortable. The coffee was strong, and the pie the best he'd ever tasted. He hadn't sat down all day, and it felt good to relax in this warm, cozy kitchen, knowing that he'd put in a good day's work. If next week went as well, he was certain he could finish the contract on time.

Caleb pushed a forkful of pie into his mouth, thinking he shouldn't stay long. "Is Amelia ready?"

Rebecca looked up and smiled. "She's asleep. I tucked her in with Johanna's Katy, who is spending the night. The two girls had a great time putting together a puzzle and playing Go Fish. That was all right, wasn't it? To let her play the card game?" Old Amish didn't play adult card games that involved betting, but in most families, simple games were acceptable.

"Go Fish." He shrugged. "I don't see why not."

"I can go get Amelia if you'd like, but I was hoping you'd let her sleep over tonight. She wanted me to ask you. Johanna and Roland are picking Katy up in the morning after breakfast and they could drop Amelia off with you. Or I could take her with me to Ruth's. We're going to make applesauce. That way, if you want to go to the shop for a few hours…"

Caleb considered. He usually worked around the farm on Saturday, but an extra half day would certainly make his deadline more doable. "If you're sure that it's no trouble," he said. "I'll pay you extra."

"Ne." Rebecca shook her head and rose gracefully from the chair. "I invited her. Another slice of pie?"

He glanced down, surprised to see that only crumbs remained on the plate. He went to hand it to Rebecca just as she reached for it, and their fingers accidently brushed each other. A tremor of sensation ran up his forearm and he inhaled sharply. Instantly he felt his throat flush. "No need," he stammered.

But she was already across the room and cutting more pie. Had she even noticed his touch? Caleb picked up the mug and downed a swallow of coffee to cover his confusion. He couldn't decide if this was way too comfortable or too uncomfortable. Somehow, he felt an invisible line had been crossed.

"Amelia can spend the night—since she's already asleep." He rose, feeling awkward. "I'll be on my way."

"But your pie?" She indicated the slice she'd just cut.

"I've had plenty." He grabbed his jacket and started for the door. "It was good. The pie. Thanks."

"You're welcome." She followed him to the porch.

"Send Amelia home with Roland and Johanna. No need for you to care for her on your weekend."

"As you like," Rebecca answered from the back door. "But I wish you'd take part of this pie home for breakfast."

"I told you," he said from the porch. "I've had enough."

"Good night, Caleb."

He heard the door close behind him and went down

the steps. In the middle of the dark farmyard, he stopped and took a deep breath. It had been nice sitting in the warm, cozy kitchen with Rebecca, having pie, listening to her knitting needles click.

Was Samuel right? Should he start thinking about finding a wife and a mother for Amelia?

As he unhitched his horse from the hitching post, he thought about the fact that his first instinct concerning Rebecca Yoder was that she wouldn't be an appropriate housekeeper and childcare provider. He should have listened to common sense.

Originally, he'd thought she was the wrong woman because of her age. He had assumed that she didn't have enough experience caring for children. At least not with a child like Amelia. He'd been right about her being the wrong one to have in his house, but maybe for the wrong reason.

Rebecca was the wrong woman to be his housekeeper because she was too…pretty. Too lively. She was…too…too much.

It had been a bad idea from the first day. What business did a respectable preacher have employing a single woman…one as pretty as Rebecca? If people weren't talking yet, they would be soon. Samuel was married to one of Rebecca's sisters. Had he been hinting that gossip was already circulating about Rebecca?

Did she have to go?

Of course, if he was going to go to the older women in the community and tell them he needed a different housekeeper, he'd need to give them a reason. Rebecca was an excellent housekeeper. He couldn't deny that any more than he could deny that Amelia liked her, and the child's behavior was improving under Rebecca's tutelage. What would he say to the women of the community?

That he was afraid that he could possibly be attracted to her? He couldn't do that. It would be completely inappropriate. He wasn't even sure it was true.

Caleb climbed up into the buggy. The one thing he did know to be true was that something had to be done about Rebecca Yoder.

Chapter Seven

"First breakfast, and then I'm sure Susanna will take you, Katy and Mae out to her library and let the three of you look at the children's books." Rebecca motioned for Amelia to take her place at the table between the other two girls.

She scrambled up into the chair, and after a burst of small female greetings and chatter, the little girls closed their eyes for a few seconds of silent grace. Once the blessing had been asked, Rebecca handed each an apple-walnut muffin, a cup of milk and sections of tangerines. "Now, who wants oatmeal?" Rebecca asked. "Mam made it this morning before she went to school."

Caleb had driven over in the buggy to drop his daughter off at the Yoder house this morning, a Wednesday, more than two weeks after the misunderstanding with Rebecca. Rebecca knew that pride was a fault, but she couldn't help being pleased with the little girl. Over the past weeks, she had come to adore Amelia. The child could be spirited, sometimes even naughty, but she had a loving heart, and she could be extremely helpful when she wanted to be. It was natural that a child raised without a mother could be difficult at times; all Amelia needed was a gentle but firm woman's guidance.

And…if Rebecca was absolutely honest with herself, she had to admit that she liked working for Caleb. Since he'd apologized for being cross with her the day Amelia pushed Mae off the step, he had been nothing but kind and pleasant. He had done as he'd said he would—he'd told other members of the community, including her mother, that he'd made a mistake in judgment and that he'd been hasty with Rebecca.

She'd been a little embarrassed that the whole incident hadn't been dropped. But at the same time, it pleased her that Caleb was true to his word, even if it meant taking public blame—something not all men were willing to do. Seeing what a good father he was and how seriously he took his church responsibilities made her admire Caleb's character even more.

Despite their awkward beginning—when he'd unnecessarily come to her rescue that evening in his barn loft—Rebecca was glad that she hadn't heeded her friends' warnings about how difficult Caleb and Amelia were. Mam was right. It was always better to form your own opinions and not listen to other people—especially when they had something unkind to say about strangers.

"Becca!" Susanna tugged at her arm. "You are not a good listener."

"*Ach,* I'm sorry. I was woolgathering." Rebecca glanced down at her sister. "What is it, honey?"

Something had clearly upset Susanna. Her nose and cheeks were red, and her forehead was creased in a frown. "Listen to me, Becca. I *said* I don't want to take the *kinner* out to my library."

Surprised at such an unusual declaration from Su-

sanna, who was always so willing to help, Rebecca
stared at her in confusion. "You don't?"

"Don't want to read books," Susanna said adamantly.
"Don't want to watch Mae, Katy and Amelia."

"But you love taking care of the library." Anna
poured milk on Amelia's oatmeal and sprinkled rai-
sins and bits of chopped apple on top. "And it's your
responsibility."

"The girls want to take home books," Rebecca reminded her. "Don't you want to show them—"

"Ne," Susanna cut her off. "I want to make applesauce with you."

At a loss for words, Rebecca glanced up. Ruth, Miriam, Anna and Johanna were all looking at Susanna,
too. They'd joined her in Mam's kitchen this morning
to make applesauce and can it for the five households.
Usually, Mam was in the center of applesauce produc-
tion, but this was a school day. The sisters had planned
to take on the task as a surprise and finish before Mam
arrived home. Naturally, Ruth, Johanna and Anna had
brought their children—the babies and those too young
for school—and everyone had expected Susanna to en-
tertain the little girls, as she always did. Small babies
were easy to feed and tuck into cradles, cribs and bas-
sinets, but active four- and five-year-olds could pose
problems during the canning process if they weren't
kept safely occupied.

"We were counting on you." Ruth smiled at Susanna.
"You know you love the girls."

"Ya." Susanna nodded her head firmly. "Love the
girls, but want to make applesauce. Today. For King
David."

Susanna's speech was sometimes difficult for strangers to understand because she had Down syndrome. It was especially hard to follow her when she switched back and forth between *Deitsch* and English indiscriminately, but Rebecca had no trouble interpreting her little sister's meaning. Most of the time, Susanna was sweet-natured and biddable, but when she made up her mind to do something, she proved she was a Yoder. Susanna could be as stubborn and unmovable as Johanna.

Rebecca looked at Anna, who just shrugged.

"Susanna wants to make applesauce." Miriam chuckled. "So I guess we go to plan B and let her help."

"Me, too," Mae piped up from the table. "I want to make applesauce."

Katy chimed in. "And me! I can help!"

"I can, too." Oatmeal dribbled from Amelia's mouth.

Rebecca grabbed a napkin and wiped Amelia's chin. Amelia slid down from her chair, and Rebecca leaned over and gave her a hug. When Amelia's arms tightened around her neck, Rebecca felt a catch of emotion in her chest. She was making real progress with Amelia. She knew she was.

"I can help," Katy repeated.

"We're happy that you all want to be big helpers," Anna assured them with a motherly smile. "But you can help most now by finishing your breakfast so we can clear away the dishes." Seemingly mollified, at least for the moment, Amelia returned to her seat and the children went back to eating.

Ruth took Susanna's hand and turned it over to show a Band-Aid. "Remember what happened when you were peeling potatoes Saturday? You cut yourself. One time you cut your hand so badly that you had to go to the hospital for stitches. That's why Mam would rather you didn't use sharp paring knives."

"We love you," Johanna put in. "We don't want you to get hurt again."

"You can help us, if you want," Anna soothed. "You can wash the apples and jars and—"

"I want to peel apples," Susanna insisted. "Me. Make applesauce for King David. He likes applesauce. With *cimmanon*."

Miriam rolled her eyes.

Rebecca sighed. The family had thought that Susanna's innocent infatuation with David King, a young man who also had Down syndrome, would pass. But to Mam's distress, and all of the sisters, it showed no signs of going away.

Amish girls grew to women and married and had families of their own. That was the way it had always been. But because sweet Susanna had been born with Down syndrome, in many ways, she would always remain a child. There would be no husband for Susanna. She would never have her own family. Her family would always be those who loved her most: her mother, her sisters and brothers-in-law, her aunts and grandmother and her nieces and nephews. Through the years, Mam had tried to explain this to Susanna, but she never understood.

The family had always cherished Susanna. Their father had called her their special blessing. If there were things Susanna couldn't do—like using sharp tools or driving a horse and buggy—God had given her special gifts. Susanna could see clearly into the hearts of others, and she possessed endless patience and compassion. Susanna had a tender understanding of children and animals, and she seemed to possess her own store of sunshine that she carried with her. Just being near Susanna and seeing her joy in everyday things made other people happier. In Rebecca's mind, Dat had been right. Susanna was not only one of God's chosen; she was a blessing to the family because they all learned so much by knowing her.

For all those reasons and a hundred more, none of them wanted to deny her the pleasure of helping in the daily household tasks. She could help in making applesauce as she helped Mam in the garden and kitchen, as she helped at community gatherings. But there were things that weren't safe for Susanna to attempt, one of which had proved to be cutting or peeling. And, until recently, Susanna had seemed to accept those limitations.

But today, apparently, was going to be different. Susanna's lower lip stuck out. She folded her chubby arms and stamped her foot. "I want to peel apples," she said.

"Sorry," Johanna said firmly. "Mam says no."

"It's up to Mam," Anna agreed. "You'll have to ask her."

"Ya," Miriam said. "And she's at school."

Tears glistened in Susanna's eyes and one slid down her cheek. Angrily, she wiped it away. "No library books," she flung at them. "No washing apples." Turning abruptly, she trudged out of the kitchen and up the stairs, leaving her sisters astonished.

"I'm sorry she's upset," Ruth said, crossing the room to check on her sleeping twins. Mam and Irwin had carried a cradle down from the attic, and when Ruth or Anna visited, there was usually a baby tucked into it. In Ruth's case, with her twin boys, there were two. "I think someone is awake and hungry," Ruth murmured.

She picked up Adam and sat down in the rocker near the window. Covering herself modestly with a shawl, she began to nurse the baby.

"It's good to have so many little ones in the house," Anna said. Her own youngest, Rose, was asleep in Hannah's bed. She wiped her hands on her apron and walked over to smile down at Ruth's other sleeping boy. "I know it makes Mam happy."

"Shouldn't one of us go up and talk to Susanna?" Johanna wiped off an already spotless counter and shifted a large kettle from one burner on the stove to another. "If she's really upset…"

"Maybe we should let her be," Ruth said. "Mam would have our heads if she had another accident with a paring knife, and once she's over her fuss, she'll be fine."

"Can we go see the books?" Amelia ventured. "Is there one about a giraffe?"

"I have a giraffe book," Mae said. "And a book about chickens."

"I want a book about ponies." Katy tugged at her mother's apron. "The brown pony with the black mane. That book."

"Come on, *kinner.*" Miriam indicated the door with a nod of her head. "I'll take you out to pick books."

Giggling excitedly, the three girls followed Miriam outside to the Amish community library, in what had once been Dat's milk house.

"And that leaves us to start on the applesauce." Anna placed her hands on her ample hips and glanced at the huge copper-bottomed pots that stood on both Mam's woodstove and the six-burner, propane gas range. "Do you two want to start carrying in the apples? We've got a lot of peeling and cutting to do before they're ready for the kettles."

"Sure," Rebecca agreed. Bushels of Black Twig, Granny Smith, Winesap and Jonathan apples waited on the porch. Making applesauce with her family was something that she looked forward to all year. She loved the heady smells of cooking apples and cinnamon, and she loved seeing the results—rows of quart jars of applesauce to line the pantry shelves. There was something so satisfying about knowing that a few days' work provided good food that would last them until next fall and the next crop of ripe fruit.

The baskets were heavy, but the Yoder sisters had done manual labor since they were young, and Rebecca didn't mind the lifting. Peeling was easy. Her fingers remembered what to do while she was free to sit and visit with her sister. They laughed and shared memories of their childhood as well as amusing or serious moments in their own homes.

This is a good day, a happy day. But how many days with my sisters do I have left?

Since Rebecca was fifteen, she'd been taking part in young people's singings and frolics. So far, while she watched her sisters, cousins and friends court and marry, she hadn't met a man with whom she wanted to spend the rest of her life.

An unmarried girl her age usually began to look farther afield; it wasn't uncommon to go to another community in another state to find a husband. It wasn't the thought of leaving her mother's house that bothered her as much as not having her sisters around her on a daily basis, as she did now. How could she marry and move away and not watch Anna's little Rose learn to talk, or see Ruth's twins start to crawl and then walk? What would she do without Miriam to tease and laugh with, or Johanna, who gave the best advice? How could she leave all those she loved to go away to be a wife and miss the remaining years of Grossmama's life?

If only there were someone here like...like Caleb.

Caleb was a fine man, of course. That went without saying. But she didn't want him for a husband. He was a preacher and too settled in his ways for her. Not old exactly, but thirty, at least.

A preacher's wife? she mused. *Impossible.* She couldn't imagine herself as a preacher's wife. The community expected a certain seriousness from the spouse of a religious leader. Dat had been Bishop and her mother had always been respected. Women came to Mam when they needed help or advice in their personal lives. Mam had always had a dignity, an instinctive manner that told even the English that she was an authority figure.

Rebecca sighed as she tossed another apple peel in the bucket. She was definitely too worldly and not humble enough to be a preacher's wife. Besides, Caleb didn't think of her as a candidate for courtship. Eventually, she knew that he would seek out a wife, but it would be some older woman, probably a widow with children. Someone Johanna's age. Johanna would have been a good match for Caleb if she and Roland hadn't fallen in love all over again and wed.

I could end up meeting some young man from Ohio or Oregon or Virginia and going to make a new life among his family and friends, Rebecca thought.

"More apples," Susanna said as she dumped a dozen washed Jonathans into Rebecca's bowl.

As Ruth had said, Susanna had gotten over her huff and come downstairs as cheerful as always. She'd taken her turn at watching the children and rocking babies and changing diapers as the rest of them had. Susanna had said nothing more about peeling apples and no one had mentioned it to her. Rebecca hoped that she'd forgotten all about it.

"So how are you and Caleb getting on?" Miriam asked Rebecca.

"Fine. I like him," Rebecca answered.

Miriam glanced at Ruth. "What we were wondering is, how much does *he* like *you?*"

Rebecca glanced around to be certain Amelia, Mae and Katy hadn't crept into the room to listen to the adults as she and Leah used to do when they were that age. "It's not like that," she said quietly. Suddenly she felt anxious. "Caleb's my employer, not my beau."

"Still, he's a good-looking man," Anna pronounced, turning from the stove where she was stirring a pot of cooking apples. "And single."

"*Very* single," Johanna agreed. She placed Luke back in the cradle beside a sleeping Adam. "You have to be careful, Rebecca. Make certain that you never give people a chance to gossip about you."

"*Ya,*" Anna agreed. She took a long-handled wooden spoon and dipped out a spoonful of cooked apples to taste. "Samuel and I were always chaperoned when we were alone together."

"Caleb is my employer." Rebecca frowned. "He's our preacher. He's the last person I'd be interested in. And he certainly hasn't shown any—"

"*Ne?*" Miriam raised her eyebrows. "I saw him

watching you at service. He didn't look all that unin-
terested to me."

Flustered, Rebecca stood up, dropping apples onto
the floor. "That's silly." She stooped to pick up the fallen
fruit. "Caleb's too old for me." One apple rolled under
the table and she had to get down on her hands and
knees to retrieve it.

"Now who's talking foolishness?" Anna said. "You're
twenty-one, and Caleb can't be much past thirty-one
or thirty-two. There's a bigger age difference between
me and Samuel." She chuckled. "And look how that
turned out."

"No one would blame you if you set your *kapp* for
him," Miriam chimed in. "Caleb Wittner is a good
catch."

"Is that what people are saying?" Rebecca rose to her
feet. She tried but couldn't keep the indignation out of
her voice. "That I've set my *kapp* for him? Because that
isn't true. He's the last man I'd want to marry."

Ruth and Johanna exchanged meaningful looks.
"That's what I said about Roland Byler," her oldest sister remarked. "Sometimes a smart woman is the last to
see what's plain as day to everyone around her."

Chapter Eight

That afternoon, Rebecca was attempting to open the outside cellar door of her mother's house while balancing a box of quart jars full of applesauce, when Caleb came around the corner of the back porch.

"You're here early." She hadn't expected him until four or so. What surprised her more was the warm pleasure she felt at seeing him unexpectedly.

"Let me take those for you," he offered. "They're heavy."

"Thanks."

It was kind of him to offer. Many men didn't do that sort of thing. They just expected their wives and daughters and sisters to manage the household tasks. Most Amish men considered the home a woman's domain, and they would be embarrassed to be caught carrying a dish or making a pot of coffee. Not that women were in any way inferior to men in their faith; men and women simply divided the daily work. Maybe their new preacher was more progressive than Rebecca had first thought.

Caleb took the case of jars, Rebecca unhooked the

latch on the door and they went down into the cellar. The dirt-floored cellar was a good place for storing potatoes, onions and rows and rows of home-canned fruit and vegetables because the temperature never dropped below freezing. Deep bins of straw held cabbage, winter squash, turnips and apples. Most English people got all of their groceries at the store, but among the Amish in their community, it was customary to buy only what couldn't be grown in a garden or purchased from neighbors.

Canning, drying and salting food was labor intensive, but Mam had taught her daughters well. Rebecca knew that when she had her own home, she would be as capable of preserving fruits, vegetables and meats as her older sisters and their mother.

"Watch your head," Rebecca warned Caleb. The old brick stairway was steep and the overhead beam low enough that he had to duck when he reached the bottom of the steps and entered the main room. Barred windows above the outside ground level let in light, but the cellar remained shadowy.

"Back here," she said, showing Caleb the way to a windowless chamber beyond the main room. She turned on a battery-powered lantern that stood on a shelf, illuminating the shelves built into the brick foundation. Quarts of applesauce already lined one shelf. On the other side of the passageway was an identical space with more shelving, and beyond that, there was another room where strings of sausage and preserved hams hung above kegs of curing sauerkraut.

"You girls have been busy," Caleb said. "Did you make all this applesauce today?"

"Ne." Rebecca began to take the jars one by one and

stand them carefully on the shelf, turning each one so that the cheerful labels faced outward. Each label bore the date and contents in her own handwriting. "This is our second batch."

"You wouldn't have any extra left over for a hungry man, would you?" he teased.

"A dozen quarts," she answered. "Waiting on the porch for you. Did you find Amelia? She was on the porch *reading* with Katy."

"I did." He smiled a slow smile that lit his eyes up. "She showed me a book about a burro. She said that she could take it home for two weeks. You don't mind?"

Rebecca shook her head and took two more jars from the box. "Oh, no. It's Susanna's library. She has books for the children...and adults. Some in the community wanted books for their little ones, but Bishop Atlee thought it best if they not borrow from the county library."

"Because not all of the Englishers' books are suitable for Amish children," he finished.

She returned his smile. "Exactly. Mam found a used bookstore, and they save books for us. We also buy books from the county library when they have their book sales. Susanna has collected more than two hundred. It makes her feel useful and it pleases the children and their families."

Caleb lowered the cardboard box as she took the last two jars from him and rested a hand against the wall. He seemed more relaxed than usual, and it made him look younger. The lines around his eyes had eased. In the shadowy light, it was easy to overlook the scars that marred his face. Rebecca wondered if they pained him, but she didn't want to ask. That seemed too forward.

"Amelia's mother hated canning," he said. "I used to help her with the tomatoes. We had a cellar in our Idaho house, the house… The one that caught fire. Our first place, though, was much smaller—only three rooms." He chuckled. "We were young and poor. That first winter, snow blew through the cracks around the kitchen window and covered our table."

"Brrr." Rebecca shivered. "That must have been tough."

"*Ya,* it was, but there were good times, too. My Dinah was an orphan, and that first house we rented, it was her first time having her own kitchen."

"Did she have other family?" Rebecca tried to imagine what Amelia's mother had been like. She must have been pretty, Rebecca thought, because Amelia was so pretty.

"A half sister and a brother in Missouri, but the sister was fifteen years older, and the brother was in a wheelchair. He had all he could do to provide for his own wife and children. Dinah was raised in an uncle's family. Six boys and no girls. Dinah had to work hard. Her aunt and uncle didn't want her to marry me because they counted on her help with the cooking and cleaning."

Rebecca didn't know what to say, so she remained silent. Caleb reached up and touched a label on one of the jars of applesauce. "Nice handwriting."

"Thank you." She averted her eyes, suddenly shy. Her fingertips tingled, and she felt a wash of warmth flow through her. She didn't want to be prideful, but she'd always taken pleasure in writing. "If you don't put what's in the jar on the label, you might get squash when you wanted beets," she said.

"Beets?" Caleb chuckled. "Beets are red. At least they were the last time I noticed."

"I guess you've never sent Irwin to the cellar for squash," she ventured.

"*Ach,* that one." Caleb's smile widened into a grin. "I saw him last church Sunday. Paying more attention to the King girl than to the sermon. He'll bear watching, that boy."

Rebecca smiled back, feeling more at ease talking about her foster brother than herself. "Mam says Irwin never seeks out mischief. It just sticks to him like flies to flypaper."

Caleb straightened one of the jars. "Samuel told me that you write more than just applesauce labels. He said that you are a regular correspondent for *The Budget.*"

The Budget was an Amish newspaper published weekly in Ohio and circulated not only nationally, but internationally. It featured stories and classified ads pertinent to Amish life, but what everyone read it for was the newsy blurbs about what was happening socially in various Amish communities.

"Guilty," she admitted. Caleb was standing very close, so close that she was very aware of how tall he was and how broad his shoulders were. She liked his hands best of all: strong hands, even the one that the fire had scarred. And he smelled good. Of Ivory soap and freshly cut wood. "Just community news... The weather, who had visitors and the announcements of new babies."

"And frolics and deaths," Caleb said. "It's not everyone who has a way with words—to write accounts of neighborhood events and make it interesting. I read what you put in about my barn raising. It was good." He stepped back. "I've been reading the Delaware news in *The Budget* since Eli first suggested I come out here, but I never knew it was you writing it. I didn't know if it was written by a man or woman." He hesitated. "You don't sign your name."

"Most contributors do," she said, meeting his intense gaze. It was curious…but was it something else? Rebecca felt a little breathless as she explained, "I started submitting to *The Budget* when I was eleven, and Mam didn't think that I should take credit because I was so young. She was afraid it would make me proud. So I got in a habit of signing Delaware Neighbor or Kent County Friend, whatever seemed right that day." She hesitated. "Why would Samuel bring up my writing to you?"

"It was an accident, really," he said. "We were talking about a farm auction listed there. Abe Hostetler's in Lancaster? Abe's a second or third cousin of mine on my mother's side. I mentioned your article to Samuel, because it told about my barn raising. That's when he said you were the one who wrote it. I was just surprised. I wouldn't have guessed."

She wasn't sure whether that pleased her or not.

His eyes narrowed as he tucked the cardboard box under his arm. "I've always considered myself a good judge of character, but you…" He shook his head. "Maybe there's more to you, Rebecca Yoder, than I first thought."

Rebecca met his gaze.

"Has the cellar fallen in on you two?" Anna's cheerful voice came from atop the cellar entrance. "I've another case of applesauce here."

"Coming," Rebecca called, breaking eye contact with Caleb, feeling off balance and not sure why.

Caleb hurried ahead of her to the stairs. "I'll take those," he called up to Anna.

Rebecca waited until he came back down the steps with another box.

"Go on up. I know where they go," he said gruffly, avoiding looking at her.

Gone was the man who'd looked at her with such intensity…the man who seemed interested in her writing. Back was her…her employer, and the moment of closeness they'd shared receded into the shadows of the cellar.

"I guess I'll go back to the kitchen for more," Rebecca said.

Anna stood, hands on hips, one eyebrow arched in suspicious curiosity when Rebecca reached the top of the steps. "A long time it took the two of you to put twelve quarts of applesauce on a shelf." Her mouth pursed. "You should take care, Rebecca. It's just us here today, but you wouldn't want others to get the wrong idea."

"We weren't doing anything wrong," she protested. "And if you doubt me, don't forget, Caleb is a preacher. He wouldn't—"

"I trust you," Anna said quietly. She leaned close and kissed Rebecca's cheek. "I know you're a good girl." She motioned toward the cellar doorway. "And Caleb seems decent, but he's a man first, a preacher second."

"We were just talking." She pushed down a small tremor of guilt. She and Caleb *had* been just talking. It was unfair of Anna to assume that anything else had taken place between them. Back stiff with indignation, she walked quickly toward the back porch. "You're beginning to sound like Aunt Martha."

Anna caught up with her and took her arm. "I'm not accusing you of anything, Rebecca. I'm just warning you to be careful. Talk all you like where people can see you or when you have Amelia as chaperone. And if he wants to ask you to walk out with him—"

"He doesn't," Rebecca insisted, shaking off her sister's hand. "He wouldn't. It's not like that. Caleb asked me about the article I wrote for *The Budget,* the one about his barn raising. Innocent enough conversation."

Anna crossed her arms over her plump figure. "Just so you keep it that way."

The hasty reply on the end of Rebecca's tongue was cut off by a scream from the barnyard. She ran into the barnyard, vaguely aware of Anna and Caleb pounding after her. *Pray God none of the children are hurt!* she thought.

But the figure at the back gate was a white-faced and breathless Dorcas. "You have to come!" her cousin shrieked. "Dat... My *dat* is..." Her words were lost in a sobbing wail.

Rebecca reached Dorcas first and grabbed her by the upper arms. Her cousin was several years older than her, but the whole family knew that she was high-strung and useless in an emergency. "What's wrong?" Rebecca demanded. "I can't help if I don't know what's happened."

Dorcas fell forward and began to wail into Rebecca's ear. "The cow. She..." Another sob. "His leg... Kicked. He's hurt."

Caleb came to a halt beside them.

"Mam's not home. You have to come," Dorcas exclaimed.

Caleb's voice was calm and steady. "How serious is his injury? Dorcas, isn't it?"

Dorcas nodded. "I don't know, Preacher. He can't get up."

"Is he conscious?" Caleb asked. "Breathing all right? Awake and talking?"

"*Ya,* he told me to run here and get someone. I think he's hurt bad."

"Dorcas, you have to calm down," Anna told her, out of breath from running. "You'll be of no use to your father in this state."

Rebecca stepped back, passing Dorcas into her sister's embrace. "Maybe we should call an ambulance?" she told Caleb.

"Ne, ne." Dorcas's hands flew into the air, fluttering like a startled bird. "No ambulance. No doctor. Mam would never agree to such an expense."

"I'll go and see how bad the injury is," Caleb said. "If he needs medical help—"

"Ne!" Dorcas shook her head and began to cry again, this time on Anna's shoulder. *"Ne,"* she repeated. "Not without my mother's say-so. I couldn't."

Caleb looked at Rebecca. "You stay here with Dorcas. My buggy and horse are still hitched up. I'll drive over to see for myself."

"He's in the barn," Dorcas managed, still in Anna's arms. "The Holstein heifer… She kicked him."

"I'm coming with you," Rebecca told Caleb. "Do you want to come, Dorcas?"

Her cousin shook her head, working her hands together. "I couldn't. It's too awful. I'll wait here."

Rebecca laid a hand on Caleb's arm. "I can show you a shortcut through the orchard. It's faster than going by the road." She glanced back at the house. "Anna and my sisters will look after Amelia. She'll be fine with them." She caught Dorcas's hand and gave it a squeeze before hurrying after Caleb.

Rebecca scrambled up into Caleb's buggy at the hitching post. He unsnapped the rope, gathered his reins and got in. In less than five minutes, Rebecca was guiding him along the back lane to the woods road that led to her uncle's farm.

Caleb drove the horse at a sharp trot. Leaves crackled under the buggy wheels and the horse's hooves thudded softly on the packed dirt. Rebecca clung to the edges of the seat, and her heart raced. *Please God, let Uncle Reuben be all right,* she prayed silently. She hoped that Dorcas was just being Dorcas, overreacting to a minor incident, but there was no way to tell.

"Money is tight for everyone, but more so for Aunt Martha and Uncle Reuben," Rebecca explained. "That's why Dorcas didn't want us to call an ambulance. But knowing her, it wouldn't be reasonable to call without seeing for ourselves first." She glanced into Caleb's face. "Sometimes Dorcas exaggerates."

"Not about something as serious as this, I would hope." His hands were firm on the reins, his back straight.

It was clear to Rebecca that he wasn't a man who jumped to conclusions or made hasty decisions. She was glad that Caleb had been at the Yoder farm when Dorcas had come. It made her feel that whatever they found at her uncle's, they would be able to deal with the situation together.

"There's a gate around the bend, just ahead," she told Caleb. "This is where Uncle Reuben's property line starts. I'll get down and open it." He nodded and she went on. "The pasture is low-lying, but if you stay on the trail you won't get stuck."

Once they were through the gate and Rebecca had closed it to keep the cows in, it was only a short distance to her aunt and uncle's barnyard, where the buildings were in various states of disrepair.

Though he had never said so, Rebecca knew her father had always thought that his sister's husband had inherited a good farm but hadn't put in the work that was needed to maintain it. Both of Martha and Reuben's sons had married young and moved to Kentucky, leaving their parents with only a daughter to help out. Uncle Reuben had always held out hope that Dorcas would find a hardworking husband to take the place in hand, but so far, that hadn't happened.

Rebecca felt a twinge of guilt that she would have such uncharitable thoughts about her uncle at such a time, but at least she hadn't expressed them to Caleb. Truthfully, she was embarrassed by the peeling paint, loose shingles and sagging doors that caused her aunt and cousin so much unhappiness. Had Uncle Reuben been ill or handicapped, his church members would have gladly come to his aid, but her uncle was as healthy as a horse. And no farmer who rose at nine and left the fields at three could expect the results of others who were more industrious.

As one of two preachers in the congregation, Uncle Reuben commanded the respect of his flock because of his position. But Rebecca had often felt that Aunt Martha's criticism of her Yoder sister-in-law, Hannah, and nieces was as much envy as an honest wish to see them live a proper Amish life. If Uncle Reuben was a better provider, maybe her aunt would be a happier person and Dorcas might have found a husband, instead of remaining single.

When they reached the main barn, Rebecca and Caleb climbed out of the buggy and she led the way inside. They had to thread through an assortment of broken tools, a buggy chassis with a rotting cover and missing wheels, bales of old, mouse-infested hay and a rusty, horse-drawn cultivator that hadn't seen a field since Rebecca was a toddler. Pigeons flew from the overhead beams and chickens scattered. A one-eared tomcat hissed at them and Rebecca cautioned Caleb not to trip over a bucket of sour milk.

"Uncle Reuben?" she called. The shed where he kept the heifers leaned at the back of the barn, but reaching it by way of the paddock would have meant walking through a morass of cow manure. This path was strewn with obstacles, but high and dry.

"Reuben!" Caleb added his strong voice to her plea. "Are you there, Reuben?"

"Here!" came a pain-filled plea. "I'm here."

Rebecca ducked beneath a leaning beam and through a low doorway cut in the barn's back wall. Her uncle lay sprawled on the dirt floor in a pile of odorous straw. The culprit, a black-and-white heifer with small, mean eyes, stood in the far corner of the shed, chewing her cud.

"Uncle Reuben!" Rebecca cried, running to kneel by his side. One leg lay at an unnatural angle. A tear in the fabric of his trousers revealed an ominous glimpse of white that Rebecca feared was a broken bone protruding through the flesh. "Oh, Uncle Reuben." She glanced back at Caleb.

He stared down at her uncle's leg. "You need to get to the hospital, Reuben." He crouched down and took the injured man's wrist. After a moment, he asked, "Anything else hurt but the leg?"

"That's enough, wouldn't you say?" Uncle Reuben snapped.

Caleb released his wrist, glanced at Rebecca, and nodding reassuringly. "Good, strong, steady pulse. Any bleeding?"

"Some. Nothing a vet can't deal with," Uncle Reuben said. "You'd be doing me a favor to call one of the Hartmans. Set this and slap some plaster on it, it'll heal well enough." His talk was bold, but Rebecca could see the pasty hue of his face and the fear in his eyes.

"You don't need a veterinarian, Reuben. You need a doctor," Caleb pronounced. "And a hospital. Likely, you'll need surgery on that leg. I'm going to go down to the chair shop and call for an ambulance."

"You'll do no such thing," her uncle said. "I've no money for—"

"No need for you to worry yourself about money right now," Caleb assured him, getting to his feet. "And no need to take chances with your leg or your life."

"I told you, I'm not paying for any English ambulance or any of their fancy doctors," Uncle Reuben insisted.

"We'll worry about the doctor bills when they come in," Caleb said. "Your neighbors will help, as I'm sure you've helped others in your community. As for the ambulance, I think you need one and I intend to see it comes for you."

"You'll ruin me! Do you know what they charge to carry you ten miles?"

"Ease your heart, Reuben." He rested his hands on his hips. "I'm making the decision, and I'll bear the cost of the transportation myself."

Chapter Nine

By nine o'clock Saturday morning, Caleb, Samuel, Eli, Charley, Roland and a half dozen other men and teenage boys were hard at work in Reuben's cornfield. A field that should have been cut a month ago. Teams were cutting the drying stalks with corn knives, a sharp-bladed tool much like a machete, and stacking them in teepee-shaped structures. The English used massive machines to harvest their fields, but in Seven Poplars, the Amish still practiced the old ways whenever possible. If the crop was to be saved, it would be due to the work of Reuben's friends and neighbors, because it would be a long time before he would be physically fit enough to do manual labor again.

As Caleb had suspected, Reuben's leg had been badly broken. Once Rebecca's uncle had reached the hospital by ambulance, he'd been examined and rushed up to surgery. Reuben was still hospitalized, but was hoping to be discharged later that day. Calling the ambulance had been the right decision. According to the EMTs who responded, any attempt to transport Reuben by buggy could have resulted in the loss of his leg or worse.

When one of the congregation became ill or injured, it was the custom of neighbors and relatives to come to his or her aid. It wasn't considered charity; it was what was expected. To do otherwise would be unthinkable in the plain community. For the next weeks, perhaps months, volunteers would tend to Reuben's livestock daily, milk the cows twice a day, finish bringing in his harvest, cut firewood and ready the farm for winter.

Caleb had spent most of Wednesday night at the hospital with Reuben and had taken off work Thursday and Friday to look after the details of seeing that his family and farm were taken care of. Somehow, because Caleb had been the first of the elders in the church to respond, it fell to him to organize assistance for Reuben's family. He'd made a schedule of regular volunteers, plus arranged for backup when the regulars couldn't be there.

Paying for the ambulance as he'd promised would cut deeply into Caleb's savings, but he had given his word. It was the right thing to do for Reuben and his family, who were—from all appearances—in reduced financial circumstances. Fortunately, Caleb had some money left over after the purchase of his farm and the expense of moving, money that had come from an unexpected inheritance. A childless uncle had died in Wisconsin, leaving his entire estate to him, making the move to Delaware possible. Helping Reuben's family seemed little enough to ask, considering the gift he had received.

Caleb fell into a steady rhythm—swing and chop, step, swing and chop, step, moving down the row. Behind him, another man gathered armfuls of corn stalks and tied them together for stacking. Cutting corn was strenuous, but Caleb didn't mind. Since he was a boy, he'd worked long, hard hours in the fields. The repetitive motion taxed the muscles, but left a man's thoughts free to roam where they would. Today, however, that might not have been a good thing.

Somehow, Caleb couldn't keep his gaze from lingering on Rebecca Yoder as she strode gracefully from one laborer to another, carrying a ladle and a bucket of cool water flavored with slices of lemon. How fine she looked this morning in her robin's-egg-blue dress, dark sweater and crisp white apron and *kapp.* Modest black stockings flashed below the hem of her full skirt as she stepped lightly over the raised rows of cut stalks, and her laughter rang merrily in the brisk fall air.

Rebecca said something to her foster brother Irwin, and Caleb heard him chuckle. As she walked away, Irwin tossed a ball of fodder at her back, and Rebecca whirled around and threw a nubbin of corncob at him. The missile struck the brim of Irwin's felt hat and knocked it off. He yelped and made an exaggerated show of retrieving it.

"Watch yourself, Irwin," Eli teased good-naturedly. "Next, you'll be getting a dipper of ice water down the back of your shirt."

"Ya," Charley agreed. His wife, Miriam, approached and he quit cutting corn to lean close and speak to her. Whatever he said must have been funny because Miriam chuckled and pushed him playfully away. Then Charley began cutting again and Miriam tied the stalks into sheaves behind him.

I miss that, Caleb thought wistfully—having a wife to share private moments and jests. Charley and Miriam were obviously a good match, despite Miriam's unusual practice of working alongside the men. The couple were strong supporters of the Gleaners, the young people's

group, and they often chaperoned or hosted youth singings. They also had strong family values. The two were
about to embark on a journey to Brazil to spend time
with Miriam's sister, Leah. Leah's husband was a Mennonite, currently serving as a missionary for his church.

It wasn't envy Caleb felt toward Charley, more a
yearning for the family happiness he had. *Maybe it was
time I started to look for another wife.* He would always
hold a special place in his heart for Dinah, but a man
wasn't meant to live without a partner. Once a suitable
period of mourning had passed, Amish communities
expected a man of his age to remarry or he was considered as going against the Ordnung.

"Thirsty?" Rebecca held up her ladle and favored
him with a big smile. A drop of water clung to the rim
of the utensil, sparkling in the sunshine. "Would you
like a drink of water?"

Startled, Caleb missed the cornstalk he'd been about
to slice off and dug into the dirt with the tip of his blade.
"*Ne...* I mean, *ya,* I would." He'd been watching Charley and Miriam and hadn't noticed Rebecca coming
up behind him.

Amusement lit her vivid blue eyes. "It's a simple
question, Caleb. Are you thirsty or not?"

"I was thinking of something else," he said. The
words came out more harshly than intended, and he
reached for the ladle. She handed it to him, but when
he brought it to his lips, he found it empty except for
a slice of lemon.

Smothering a giggle, she pursed her lips and offered
the bucket. He frowned and then scooped up some water
and drank. Without saying anything more, he helped
himself to a second dipperful. His face felt hot, but

the water was marvelously cool in his throat, and by the time he'd swallowed the last drop, he'd regained his composure. "What did you say to Irwin to set him off?" he ventured, trying to think of something, anything, other than how her rosy lips curved into such a sweet smile.

"I asked him if he knew how to catch a blue hen."

Caleb waited, the back of his neck feeling overly warm, obviously the result of the bright sunshine. There were at least a dozen workers in the field, but it seemed as if he and Rebecca were all alone. He was acutely aware of just how vibrant and attractive a young woman Rebecca was.

She chuckled. "How else? A blue chicken net."

"A joke." Not smiling, he handed back the ladle.

She chuckled and shrugged. "Guilty."

He'd noticed that she sometimes told funny stories to the children and women at church Sunday meals. And more than once, he'd caught sight of Rebecca using her handkerchief to make a hand puppet to amuse Amelia during service. Come to think of it, Amelia had been regaling him with rhymes, word teasers and silly jokes in the evenings. He didn't have to look far to see where they'd come from. "You like to make people laugh?"

She rested the dipper in the bucket and used her free hand to tuck a stray lock of bright auburn hair behind her ear. Golden freckles sprinkled her nose and cheeks, freckles that made her look younger than her actual years. "Chores go easier with a light heart," she replied.

A light heart... Caleb suddenly felt as if it was hard to breathe. He cleared his throat and stepped away from her, rubbing his free hand against his pant leg.

It was a mistake to be drawn in by Rebecca's winsome ways and easy laughter. She wasn't the woman for him. She was too young…too pretty…too sprightly. A woman like Rebecca would never want a man like him. Certainly not with his scars…or his past. He'd not been able to save Dinah. Surely that made him unworthy of a woman like Rebecca.

What he needed was a more sensible wife, one more suited to a staid and practical preacher. "*Danke* for the water," he managed. "I can't stand here lazing when there's half a field to do."

A pink flush colored her fair complexion. "I'll leave you to your work then, Preacher Caleb." Back straight, *kapp* strings trailing down her neck, she moved away, leaving him oddly disconcerted.

Caleb began to swing the corn knife again, slashing with hard, quick blows that left a sharp line of stalk stubble behind him. *Ya,* he decided, he had put this off far too long. It was time a new wife came to fill his loneliness and tend his motherless daughter. Too long he'd clung to his grief for Dinah. She was safe in God's hands, free from all earthly pain and care, and it was his duty to pick up the reins of his life and carry on.

"What was that… You and Caleb?" Miriam whispered.

Rebecca and Miriam had returned to Aunt Martha's kitchen to help the other women set out the midday meal. Rebecca was slicing meatloaf, and Miriam had stepped close to her, a platter of warm *kartoffel kloesse,* potato croquettes, in her hand.

Rebecca's eyes widened. "What do you mean, me and Caleb?"

Miriam elbowed her playfully in the side. "Come

on, it's me. I know you too well. Don't try to pretend you don't know what I'm talking about. I saw the two of you together in the field. You like him, don't you?"

Rebecca put down the knife, glanced around to be sure no one was watching them and pulled her sister into the pantry. "Do you want everyone to hear you? I took him water like I did every other man."

Miriam shook her head and chuckled as she set the platter on the counter in the pantry. "*Ne,* little sister. Not like every other man. If my Charley looked at you like Caleb did… Well, let's say he'd better not if he knows what's good for him."

The pantry was shadowy, the only light coming from a narrow window. High shelves filled with jars of canned fruit and vegetables lined the walls, and a wooden bin held cabbages, potatoes, onions and carrots. Aunt Martha was not known for her housekeeping skills, but this one room was always clean…if you didn't notice the cobwebs overhead or the fingerprints on the windowpanes.

"There's nothing between us."

"So why does he look like a lovesick calf and why are your cheeks as red as pickled beets every time his name is mentioned?" Miriam asked. She hesitated. "You know, he's perfectly acceptable, if you do like him. I could have Charley talk to him. He could—"

"What would make you say such a thing?" Rebecca grabbed her sister's hand. "Caleb hasn't said anything that would make me believe… At least, I don't think…" She let go of Miriam's hand and let her words trail off as she remembered the strange sensations she'd felt when she and Caleb had exchanged words in the cornfield.

Excitement made her giddy. Maybe it hadn't been

her imagination. If Miriam had noticed the way Caleb looked at her…then maybe it wasn't just her own foolish fancy. Maybe he did like her.

Miriam planted a hand on her hip. "Do you like him or not?"

"I don't know," she blurted, looking up at her. "I think… Maybe I do…but…"

"He wouldn't be my choice for you," Miriam remarked. "He's too serious, too stuffy."

"Caleb isn't stuffy. He is serious at times, but he has a lighthearted side, too. You should see how he plays and laughs with Amelia. And he's had so many sorrows in his life. Can you blame him if he's sad sometimes?"

"The scars on his face? His hand? They don't bother you?"

Rebecca shook her head, thinking. "It's odd to hear myself even say it, but the truth is…I don't notice them. He has such nice eyes, and—"

"You don't *notice* them," Miriam groaned. "One half of his face and you don't see it." Then she smiled. "You've got it bad. I can have Charley talk to him and see what's what."

A little thrill passed through Rebecca. "Charley would do that for me?"

"Of course he would."

"Even if you don't think he would be a good choice for me?"

Miriam smiled kindly. "Love is love, little sister. There were some who would have chosen John over Charley for me…."

"But Charley was the right husband for you," Rebecca finished.

"He was. So say the word and I'll have Charley speak

with Caleb. Of course, if he's interested in getting to know you to see if you might be a suitable match, different arrangements will have to be made with your job. It wouldn't be seemly for you to be working at the preacher's house and courting him at the same time."

Courting Caleb? Just the sound of the words made Rebecca nervous…and a little giddy. Was that what she wanted? Was that the direction God was leading her? She looked at her sister. "Let me pray about it for a day or two. It's too soon—"

"You know Mam would like it if you married close to home, and we all love little Amelia." Miriam chuckled softly. "Of all my sisters, you're the last one I'd expect to be a preacher's wife."

"I said I'd pray on it," Rebecca answered. "I'm not going to rush into anything. And don't you dare tell Anna or Johanna or—"

"I know, I know." Miriam grinned. "I'll keep your secret, but don't wait too long. A lot of mothers would consider Caleb Wittner a good catch for their daughters. You wait too long to make up your mind and someone could snatch him right out from under you."

When the dinner bell rang, Caleb walked back to the Coblentz house with the other men. As he approached, he couldn't help noticing that one of the back porch posts was leaning and the rails, on their last legs, were sagging. He climbed the rickety steps, thinking that while Reuben was laid up with his injury, it wouldn't hurt to have some of the neighbors do some work on his house. It pained him to think that a family in his church was living like this when others were clearly doing so much better financially.

Someone had set up a tub of water, a bar of soap and towels on the porch. Charley and Eli were there cleaning up. Charley was laughing at some nonsense and shaking his wet hands, splattering a protesting Eli with soapy drops of water. As they stepped aside, still teasing each other, Caleb pushed up his sleeves and washed his hands thoroughly. When he reached for a towel, Martha's daughter, Dorcas, handed him a clean one.

"It's good of you to come and help us. Get in our corn," Dorcas said. She was a tall, spare woman, plain in features, but with good skin. Unmarried, he remembered, and probably nearing thirty. He'd not exchanged more than a few words with her since her father's accident, and not many since he'd come to Delaware.

"I'm glad to help," he answered.

She covered her mouth with her hand and offered what he thought might be a smile. Had he ever seen her smile? No matter, she was obviously a devout and modest young woman, and it would do no harm to consider her in his search for a prospective bride.

Dorcas's mother, Martha, appeared at his side and tugged at his sleeve. He turned toward her. *"Ya?"*

"A word, if you would, Preacher Caleb." She smiled, showing sparkling white, obviously artificial uppers.

Caleb glanced into the kitchen where the other men were taking seats at the long table. "Maybe after the meal? I think Samuel is about to—"

"Of course," Martha agreed. "After you've eaten. Actually, Grace Hartman, my niece… She's Mennonite. My brother's daughter. Not raised among us. Offered a ride to the hospital. If you'd like to join Dorcas and me to visit Reuben. He's not to come home until tomorrow now. Nothing to worry about. Just a slight fever. Such a terrible accident, a man of his years. So glad you were there to come to his aid in his time of—"

"The grace," Caleb reminded her. "The others are waiting."

"After the meal," Martha repeated, patting his arm. "You are more than welcome to—"

"It's kind of you to ask," Caleb replied, glancing toward the kitchen door. "But we need to finish that field today. The weather forecast calls for rain tomorrow night, and—"

"Tomorrow being the Sabbath, there will be no work," Martha finished for him. "*Ya,* you are right to remind me. My Reuben is such a devout member of the church, and we've tried to raise our Dorcas to be equally obedient to the rules of our community." Creases crinkled in the corners of her eyes as she beamed at him. "She's quite accomplished, our Dorcas. You've noticed her, I'm sure. As you would, a single man, a widower with a young daughter in need of a mother."

Caleb nodded. He could feel the impatient gazes of hungry men on him.

"No need to hold you back from your meal," Martha said. "You've worked so long and hard in the field today. You've earned your rest and a full stomach. But I wondered, if we can't talk today, perhaps tomorrow evening. Supper. Bring your daughter, naturally. Reuben will be home. We would be honored to have you. Six o'clock?"

"*Ya,*" Caleb agreed. "Six." He saw his opportunity and nearly bolted for the door. "Tomorrow." Three long strides and he was in the kitchen.

"About time," Charley grumbled. "We're starving."

Caleb slid into the only empty chair and closed his eyes.

"Let us give thanks," Samuel intoned.

When their silent prayers ended and they opened their eyes, the serious eating began. Biscuits, potato dishes and creamed celery were passed around. Women slid more bowls of vegetables and meats onto the patched white tablecloth.

Dorcas placed a bowl of gravy down with a thump directly in front of Caleb's plate. "For the meatloaf," she said. "My mother made it." Again, she smiled behind her hand.

He nodded, wondering exactly what he'd committed to by agreeing to come to supper. He had been able to tell by the look in Martha's eyes that she had more on her mind than a simple thank-you supper. But maybe this was God's plan for him. Maybe finding a new wife wouldn't be that difficult. He didn't know anything about Dorcas, but that was what courtship was all about.

"Lord, help me," he murmured silently. But as he glanced up, he saw Rebecca leaning over the table and pouring water into Eli's glass tumbler. And just for a second, he absently stroked the scar on his cheek and wished...

"Don't go far," Rebecca called to Amelia. "I just need to get an armload of kindling for the wood box."

The little girl and Fritzy were racing back and forth between the woodshed and the house. Amelia was throwing a leather ball Charley had sewn for her out of old scraps into the air. The dog would jump up and catch it in his mouth, and then the child would chase him. The big poodle ran in circles around her as she shrieked with laughter and tried to catch him to get the ball back. Only when Amelia stopped, breathless, would Fritzy drop the toy at her feet. Then the game would begin all over again.

With a final glance over her shoulder to see that dog and girl were where they were supposed to be, Rebecca entered the shed and began gathering small pieces of wood for the stove. She had almost all she could carry, then stooped to pick up one last piece. As she reached for it, she heard the door hinges squeak behind her.

She looked back and saw the tall silhouette of a man in the doorway. Startled by Caleb's sudden appearance, she stepped sideways onto a log and lost her balance. She quickly righted herself, but in the process lost control of the kindling, spilling half of it back onto the floor.

"I didn't mean to frighten you." Caleb stepped forward to steady her. "I'm sorry."

"*Ne,* it's nothing." She could feel the blood rising in her face. "I just…" Clumsily, she began to gather up the wood. "You just surprised me."

"Let me," he insisted, taking the wood from her arms. "The fault is mine. I thought I left the wood box full."

"I didn't realize it was so late." Rebecca kept her face turned away as she picked up some bigger pieces of wood. Caleb must think she was flighty, to be so startled by his arrival in his own woodshed. "Supper is on the back of the stove," she said.

Caleb carried his armload outside and she followed, carrying the additional logs she'd picked up. "I may be a little early," he said. "I finished the trim work for that fireplace surround I was telling you about, the fancy one with the columns. They want me to come to Lewes and mount it on-site. They're even going to pay for my driver."

"That's good," Rebecca said. The town in Sussex County had an area where old houses were being moved in and restored. A contractor had contacted Caleb about doing specialty pieces for some of his projects. It was different than the way he usually worked, but Caleb seemed pleased. He said the pay was twice what he normally made. Rebecca was happy that the English people realized what a craftsman Caleb was. Secretly, she was sure that, preacher or not, he took pride in his woodwork.

"I wanted to tell you that I'll be going out for supper on Wednesday. You won't have to make anything for us that night," Caleb said.

"Oh?"

"*Ya,* to Reuben and Martha's."

Again? Rebecca tried not to let the surprise she felt show. "Oh." Once was natural, after all that Caleb had done for her aunt and uncle, but he'd already had dinner with them on Sunday. Twice in one week? An uneasy thought rose in Rebecca's mind. "You and Aunt Martha and Uncle Reuben and…and Dorcas." She heard Fritzy barking and Amelia's squeal of laughter. The game was still going on. But the two seemed a long way off. Supper twice in one week usually meant…

"Caleb, are you courting my cousin?" she blurted out, louder than she intended.

He stopped short, turned and fixed her with that intense, dark stare. He suddenly looked as uncomfortable as she felt. "We're not courting, Dorcas and I. At least, not yet."

Rebecca was stunned. She gripped the wood, her fingers numb. "Not yet?" she repeated.

Only Saturday she had had the conversation with Miriam about the possibility of having Charley speak to Caleb about her. When Rebecca had said she wanted to pray about it first, Miriam had warned her not to wait too long, or someone else might snatch him up. But Dorcas?

Rebecca realized how uncharitable such a thought was. Why not Dorcas? She was the single daughter of a preacher. It was perfectly logical that she and Caleb would have much in common, wasn't it?

"We're trying to see if we're compatible," Caleb explained. "To find out if we want to walk out with each other." His eyes narrowed. "Why? Is there something wrong with Dorcas?"

"Ne, ne," she said quickly. She looked down at the frozen ground, feeling a sense of loss and not entirely sure why. She had prayed about Caleb, but she'd gotten no answer. Had Charley been standing here at this moment, ready to speak with Caleb about her, she wasn't sure she would have agreed to it. "She's a good girl, Dorcas. Very…"

Caleb cocked his head slightly. "Very what?"

Frantically, Rebecca searched her mind for something positive and truthful to say in her cousin's defense. "She's devout. And she's a dutiful daughter. Thoughtful and obedient to her parents."

"Admirable in anyone."

"Ya," Rebecca continued in a rush. "A hard worker, not lazy. And she makes good chowchow. The best. Everyone says so. She sells a lot of it to the Englishers at their stand at Spence's."

He chuckled. "A handy skill to have, I suppose. A good thing I have always been fond of chowchow."

Rebecca quickened her step, hurrying past him to the back porch and into the house. She dumped her load into the wood box beside the stove. Caleb came into the kitchen with Amelia and Fritzy on his heels. "Do you want me to stay and keep Amelia on Wednesday?" she asked him. "Or take her to Mam's?"

"I considered taking her. It's important to me that Amelia be comfortable with any young woman I care to…to consider as a wife."

"Naturally," Rebecca dusted her hands off on her skirts. She was trying not to be upset. What right did she have to be? If she'd been interested in Caleb, she should have spoken up sooner.

"But maybe I should wait. Courting is a big step." He dumped his own load into the box. "It isn't one I would take lightly. But I think it is time. Amelia should have a mother." He paused, and then his gaze met hers again. "And maybe it's time I stopped mourning Dinah and took a new wife."

Rebecca forced herself to smile and nod. "It is only right," she agreed. "A preacher should…" She took a breath. "Amelia does need a mother. Every child does." Her voice softened and she looked away. "You'll do what is right for her, Caleb. You always do."

Chapter Ten

The following Saturday, Rebecca, Ruth and Miriam went to Fifer's Orchard in the nearby town of Wyoming to get apples. They were picking from the seconds bins by the side of the building and chatted while they worked. It was the last chance they'd have to spend with Miriam for a while as she and Charley were headed to Brazil to spend time with Leah and Daniel that week, and would be gone almost a month.

Mam's orchard hadn't produced many sound apples this year, and despite the quarts and quarts of applesauce they'd put up, Mam wanted more fruit for apple pies and cakes and apple butter. They would purchase baskets of the best apples to store in the cellar for winter, but the slightly bruised or odd-shaped seconds would be fine for cooking.

"So I heard Caleb's courting Dorcas." Miriam propped her hands on her hips. "*Our cousin,* Dorcas? How did that happen?"

Rebecca glanced at Ruth and Miriam. She didn't want to talk about this with her sisters, and she certainly didn't want to talk about it in public. It had not been a good week. When Caleb had told her he was having supper with Uncle Reuben's family with the intention of trying to find out if he and Dorcas might be a suitable match, she'd been taken by surprise. Then, as the week had passed, she'd found herself growing more and more upset by the idea. And more certain she *did* have feelings for Caleb. Miriam had warned her she had to act fast, but it had never occurred to her that she'd have to act *that* fast. Even before she'd had the opportunity to consider what she felt, everything changed.

Ruth placed two apples into her brown paper bag. "I heard he went to supper at Aunt Martha's Sunday evening and again on Wednesday. Wearing his good coat. Sounds like courting to me."

"If Dorcas can land the new preacher, it will be a triumph for Aunt Martha," Miriam said. "She told Mam that she was afraid she'd have Dorcas on her hands forever."

"Mmm." Ruth picked up an apple, examined it and then rejected the apple. "Maybe it's the new tooth."

"Getting that broken tooth repaired certainly didn't hurt Dorcas's appearance," Miriam agreed. "You know I hate it when a woman's looks are more important than how beautiful she is inside, but Dorcas can use all the help she can get."

"That's not very charitable," Ruth admonished.

"I didn't mean it unkindly." Miriam looked up at her. "But the truth is, Dorcas is plain, and the way Aunt Martha insists she dress doesn't help. Amish men aren't all that different from any other. Most of the time, they'll pick the pretty girls first."

Ruth frowned. "It didn't stop our Anna from making a good match with Samuel. Her size didn't mean a thing to him."

"*Ya,* but who wouldn't want Anna? She has the biggest heart of any of us. She's a wonderful mother to Samuel's children—and she makes him happy. Not to mention that she's a better cook than even Mam."

"I think Dorcas could have married long ago if she took a page from Anna's book. It's no secret that Dorcas isn't always pleasant to be around. She can be..." Ruth nibbled at her lower lip "...critical, and..."

"Aunt Martha-ish?" Miriam suggested. "Maybe that's what Caleb is looking for. No one can fault Dorcas's devotion to the church. It could be that she's exactly the kind of wife Caleb is looking for."

Rebecca continued to sort apples and tried not to listen to her sisters. Then she tried to pretend that she didn't care whom Caleb was walking out with. If he chose her cousin, though... She swallowed, trying to dissolve the knot in her throat. Over the years, she and Dorcas hadn't always been the best of friends, but Dorcas was family and she was a member of their church. If Caleb asked Dorcas to marry him, Rebecca would have to find a way to be happy for them.

Ruth lowered her voice and moved closer to Rebecca. "You see Caleb every day. Did he say something to you about being interested in Dorcas?"

Rebecca didn't look up at her. "He said that he was visiting to see if he and Dorcas suit each other."

"Catch." Miriam tossed Rebecca an oversize green apple. "There's still time, little sister. I think you should let Charley speak to Caleb for you."

Rebecca felt tears sting the backs of her eyelids.

Ruth squeezed Rebecca's arm and looked at her. "You do care for him, don't you?"

Rebecca opened her mouth to answer, but before she could say anything, Susanna trotted down the wooden ramp toward them, waving a vegetable peeler.

"Look what I bought!" Susanna exclaimed. "With my own money. A peel-er. Now I can help peel apples. I won't cut myself." She thrust the green-handled utensil in Ruth's face. "Isn't it pretty?"

"It is." Ruth smiled back at her. "Where did you find such a good one?"

"By the reg-i-ter. King David's Mam. I saw her. Inside." Susanna was so excited that she was practically bouncing from one black athletic shoe to the other. "She helped me count my money."

"Great," Rebecca agreed, glad for a reason to change the subject. "Mam will be proud of you."

"Good job," Miriam said, admiring Susanna's purchase. "You didn't forget about wanting to peel apples, did you?"

"*Ne.* I didn't forget. I want to help," Susanna said. "Not just play with *kinner*. Help like you."

"We can always use another pair of hands," Ruth said.

Susanna nodded vigorously. "And…and when King David and me get married—" she took a deep breath "—I can make applesauce for him!"

Rebecca met Miriam's gaze, and suddenly their little sister's happy moment became a sad one for the older sisters. No matter how many peelers she bought, they all knew Susanna would never be able to marry and leave home. She would always live with Mam or one of them, and in some ways, she would always remain a child.

I should be ashamed of myself, Rebecca thought. Instead of being upset by Caleb's attention to her cousin, she should be thanking God that she wasn't born with Susanna's burden. Her sister was a precious and innocent soul, but she could never be a wife or a mother. *Someone, somewhere will surely ask me to be his wife.*

"Hi!" Grace joined them at the apple bins. "I didn't know you were coming here today. I could have picked you up in my car. I'm so glad I got to see you again before you and Charley set off on your adventure." She kissed Miriam on the cheek and continued greeting each of her sisters affectionately. Because Grace was Mennonite, she didn't wear Amish clothing, but she was dressed in a long denim skirt, a modest blouse and a lace prayer cap.

"How's school?" Rebecca asked. Grace was attending a college program for veterinary technicians and would soon be working beside her husband John at his animal hospital.

"Tough, but I love it." Grace flashed her a grin. "This one teacher I have is a real bear, but I can always count on John to help me study for her tests. I don't know what I'd do without him."

"You couldn't have found a better partner," Miriam said.

Miriam and John had been good friends for years, and she'd come close to marrying him. But he wasn't Amish, and in the end, Miriam had chosen Charley and remained true to her faith. *It was funny how things turned out,* Rebecca mused. Who would have believed that John was destined to be her brother-in-law, not by wedding Miriam as everyone expected, but by becoming the husband of a beloved half sister who'd recently come into their family? Proof that God truly had a plan for each of them.

She wondered what His plan was for her.

I thought it might have been Caleb, she thought with a pang of sadness. She'd been so certain that there was no hurry, no reason to rush the awakening feelings that stirred in her heart. Now, selfishly, she didn't want Caleb to become her cousin by marriage. She wanted more....

"So what's new at home?" Grace asked. "I kept thinking about all of you on Thanksgiving. Uncle Albert ordered a whole turkey dinner from a restaurant, and we all sat around and stuffed ourselves. Grandpa Hartman ate most of a sweet-potato pie all by himself."

"We missed you, too," Ruth said. "It was a quiet day of prayer and fasting for us."

"But we'll expect you all for Christmas dinner." Rebecca added one last apple to the bag. "Uncle Albert and his father, too."

"We wouldn't miss it. You know how 'Kota loves to play with his cousins." Grace picked up a bag of apples. "Let me help you load these in the buggy."

Ruth and Susanna went inside to pay while Rebecca, Miriam and Grace walked across the parking lot to the hitching rail.

"What's this I hear about Caleb Wittner and Dorcas?" Grace asked as they approached the buggy. "Is he really courting her? I thought that you..." Grace gave Rebecca a meaningful look. "You know. So I was surprised when John said that Noodle Troyer said—"

"Caleb isn't walking out with Dorcas." Rebecca shoved her bag of apples into the back of the buggy so hard that the brown paper split and apples spilled out and rolled across the floorboards.

Miriam chuckled. "Bad subject, Grace. I was just telling Rebecca last weekend that if she thought she might be interested in Preacher Caleb, I should have Charley speak to him before someone else beat her to him."

Rebecca whirled around. "If Caleb and Dorcas are suited to each other, I'd be the last person to—" She bit down on her lower lip.

Grace's eyes clouded with compassion. "I'm sorry. I didn't mean to…" She sighed. "It's just that…" She shrugged. "I don't understand. I'm a Yoder, and I should have learned all this stuff by now, but how the Amish choose a husband is just…just…"

"It must sound strange to you, being raised among the English," Miriam offered, "but it isn't odd to us. It's just the way things have always been done. What is it that you aren't clear about?"

"When John and I started to be interested in each other, we…we dated, sort of. He asked me out." She looked from Miriam to Rebecca. "John said that Amish boys don't ask girls to go out with them—they have someone else ask."

Rebecca nodded. "There's often a go-between. Amish boys are shy."

"Usually more so than the girls," Miriam put in. "And since our church is one of the more conservative, we like to see couples who are walking out be with other people, not alone."

"Chaperoned?" Grace said. "Even at Dorcas's age? Really?"

Miriam slid her bag in and began to gather the apples that had spilled out of Rebecca's bag before raising her gaze to meet Rebecca's. "I wanted to have Charley talk to Caleb to see how he felt about Rebecca. When there's a friend or relative asking, it's less embarrassing if the other person isn't interested."

"So Caleb had a go-between to ask Dorcas—" Grace began.

Rebecca shook her head. "*Ne.* Not exactly. Aunt Martha invited him to supper. What they are doing is visiting to see how they get along, if they want to court."

"And if they do like each other in that way, will they start going to singings and work frolics together?" Grace asked.

Miriam shrugged. "I doubt it. Both of them are older, and Caleb's been married before. I suppose the first thing people will notice is him driving her home from church services. And Caleb will keep visiting her at home."

"When Samuel was courting Anna," Rebecca said, "they went to a taffy pulling she wanted to go to, so he took her. What a disaster. Of course, the age difference isn't so great between Caleb and Dorcas. But neither of them seem the kind to want to go to young people's frolics."

Grace wrinkled her nose. "It doesn't seem very romantic."

"It's complicated." Miriam knotted the loosening ties of her blue wool scarf under her chin. "Respect, devotion to the faith and an ability to help the partner. That's what's important." She smiled. "As Grossmama always says, 'Kissing don't last. Cooking do.'"

"Maybe it's best I didn't become Amish," Grace said thoughtfully. "I married John because I loved him—

because I couldn't live without him. Respect and friendship alone wouldn't be enough for me."

And maybe not for me, either, Rebecca thought. *I think I'd rather stay an old maid than settle for a man I couldn't love with my whole heart.*

"Are you almost done?" Amelia pleaded from the bale of hay where Caleb had placed her a half hour ago.

Caleb shook his head. "Just a little while yet. Stay where you are and play with your baby."

They'd been on the way to Dover to the hardware store, but he'd stopped at Reuben's farm long enough to see if the volunteers had come by for morning milking and chores. They had, but Martha had seen him and asked if he'd clean out the horse stall. By the time he finished, he'd be in no shape to be seen in public. He couldn't help wondering when Reuben had last cleaned it.

Caleb looked down at his shoes. They'd need a good polish before tomorrow's worship. Had he known he'd be pressed into service, he'd have brought along his muck boots.

"Dat, I'm hungry."

"You're not hungry. You had soup and a chicken sandwich before we left home." Rebecca never left on Friday afternoon without leaving food for the weekend. He didn't know how he and Amelia had managed without her. She didn't just cook and clean and look after Amelia, she was tackling bigger projects, too. She was working her way through the moving boxes that had been scattered throughout the house, unpacking his life and putting it in order.

"Dat, I want to go. I'm tired of sitting here. And I need you to tie Baby's bonnet strings."

Caleb emptied another hayfork full of dirty straw and manure into the wheelbarrow. "Not now, Amelia. I'm working." The soft rag doll that Dinah had made for her was his daughter's greatest treasure. She spent hours taking the doll's clothes off, putting them on and trying to tie the tiny bonnet strings. Usually, he ended up tying them for Amelia, but in minutes, she'd have them untied and the bonnet off again.

"I can tie them for her," came a thin voice from the shadows.

Startled, Caleb almost dropped his pitchfork. *Dorcas.* He hadn't known that anyone else was in the barn. She was standing only a few feet away. How long had she been watching him and how had she gotten behind him without him seeing her?

"Ne," Amelia whined. "I want Dat to do it." His daughter clutched the doll and bonnet against her chest. "I want Dat!"

"Amelia," he chastised. She was never on her best behavior around Dorcas or her family. And to Dorcas's credit, she'd shown more patience than was warranted. "Let Dorcas fix it for you."

"Ne. Don't want her to play with my doll. It's mine."

Caleb thrust his pitchfork into the muck. "Behave yourself, child. That's no way to talk to Dorcas."

"Mam says she's spoiled." Dorcas leaned on the upright post at the corner of the stall. "She says it's to be expected. Her having no mother to teach her right."

"Do so have a mother!" Amelia flung back. "Rebecca says so. My Mam is in heaven!"

Caleb frowned at her, and Amelia's face crumpled.

"My mother says…" Dorcas began.

Her shrill monotone grated on his ears and her next words were lost to him as he stuck the pitchfork into another clump of rotting straw.

I should be ashamed of myself, he thought. Dorcas isn't responsible for the nature of her voice anymore than the color of her eyes. She had nice eyes. They were her best feature. There was nothing flashy about her face or hair, but that wasn't what a man should be looking for in a wife.

Dorcas came from a respectable family, and she was modest and hardworking, according to Martha.

If Dorcas lacked somewhat in her cooking skills, that would come in time. Amelia's mother hadn't been the world's best cook when he'd first married her, but in time she'd improved. It was unfair to compare Dorcas's chicken stew to the one that Rebecca had put on his table this week. Rebecca had tucked it neatly into a golden brown piecrust, and it had been so good that he'd finished the last slice of it for breakfast this morning. Maybe, if he suggested it, Dorcas could ask Rebecca for her recipe.

Dorcas was kind to Amelia, and if Amelia was slow to respond, it was her nature. She spent every weekday with Rebecca; it was only natural that she had become so attached to her. Amelia was constantly telling him of new games Rebecca had taught her, and silly songs they'd sung.

Caleb almost groaned out loud. What was wrong with him? Why was he thinking of Rebecca Yoder when he should be paying attention to the very suitable young woman standing behind him? Rebecca would never be interested in him. It was Dorcas's good points he should be concentrating on. On the whole, she was a fine prospect for marriage. She was clean, reasonably intelligent and she seemed interested in him. And if she had a few minor traits that rubbed him the wrong way, doubtless she could find plenty of fault with him, as well.

"Caleb."

"*Ya*, Dorcas?" He had only a small corner of the stall to go. If he finished up quickly, he might have time to go home, change and still get to the hardware store before the afternoon got too late.

"My mother is out of sugar and cinnamon. She asked if you could take me to Byler's to get some. With Dat being so poorly, we can't get to the store."

"You don't drive the horse and buggy?" He shouldn't have said that, but the words just came out before he thought.

"*Ne*. Not me. I'm afraid of horses. Dat always drives. Mam does, sometimes, when we go someplace without him, but she has a sore throat. She doesn't want to go out of the house. And she needs cheese for casserole. For the midday meal. At meeting tomorrow. Mam says..."

"*Ya*, I can take you." She kept talking while he concentrated on the last of the stall. He would spread fresh straw when he was finished. The hardware store errand could wait. He probably had enough nails to finish the pigpen anyway. If Dorcas could take Amelia into Byler's with her, the child would be satisfied that she didn't get to go to Dover today.

"...eat supper with us tonight," Dorcas was saying. "I made snapper soup. We had a big old turtle that Dat caught in the pond. He put it in a barrel and we fed it table scraps and corn and..."

Caleb stiffened. Snapper soup? Snapping turtle? His

stomach turned over. "Thank your mother," he said. "But I've stuffed peppers waiting at home. Another time, Dorcas."

He couldn't abide snapper soup. The bishop's wife had served it at the first meal he'd shared with them, and he'd forced it down and been nauseous all that night. It was a little embarrassing, being a man who didn't like the strong tastes of some traditional Amish foods.

Caleb shook off a shudder. He'd told Rebecca about his ordeal at Bishop Atlee's table one morning when they'd seen a snapping turtle crossing the road. Rebecca had laughed at the tale, but despite her teasing, he was certain that she would never invite him to share a pot of snapper soup.

"It's all right, Caleb," Dorcas went on, apparently picking up on his distaste. "We've got pigs' knuckles with sauerkraut and dumplings left over from Wednesday night's supper. You can eat that. It's still *gut.*"

Wonderful, Caleb thought with dark humor. Pigs' knuckles were his second-most-hated food and he'd already lived through that experience once this week. *What will she and Martha serve me next? Blood sausage?*

Chapter Eleven

Tuesday evening, snowfall dusted the ground with a fine layer of white. The air was cold on Caleb's cheeks as he swung his legs over the rail fence that bordered his property. He was late coming home tonight, but he was so close to finishing a console bracket that he'd lost track of the time. It was the first time he'd attempted such an intricate design and he was greatly pleased with the results.

He knew a man of faith shouldn't be guilty of *hochmut,* but when a seasoned block of oak, cherry or walnut took shape under his hands and became an object of beauty, it was hard not to feel pride in his craft. And foolishly, he wanted to show it to Rebecca. In a way, she was partly responsible for the success of the piece, because if he didn't feel confident that Amelia was safe and well cared for, he couldn't have concentrated on his work.

Snow crunched under Caleb's feet and he began to sing an old hymn of praise. His voice was nothing beyond adequate, but with only the wind and the trees to hear him, he could open his heart and sing praise. As he walked and sang, it came to him that today he was truly happy for the first time in years. Coming East had been the right thing to do for him and his daughter. It had given them the new start that they'd needed to pick up their lives and move forward. This community was quickly becoming his own, and the conservative views and practices seemed right for him.

Thank You, God, he thought. *Thank You for guiding me to a safe place when my eyes were blinded by tears.*

He slipped a hand inside his leather bag and ran his fingers over the perfect curves of the pendant at the bottom of the bracket he had made. It was shaped like a child's top and sanded as smooth as glass. Later, someone would attach the bracket to a house and probably paint it in the garish colors that the Englishers favored, but for now, it was a deep red oak with lighter streaks of shading. It was strange how his craftsmanship had improved in the months and years since the fire. It was almost as if the flames had burned away his flesh, exposing ugliness but leaving him with a greater ability to create beauty in wood.

Caleb pushed back the wave of sadness that threatened to suppress his good mood. Those times were past, and the uncle and aunt who'd cared for him had been fair. From them he'd learned to be strong, to depend on himself and to be content with few material goods—all qualities that prepared him to be a good father.

And husband?

He grimaced. Tomorrow evening would be another strained visit at the Coblentz home. He wished that he could spend some time alone with Dorcas, to really get to know her, but Martha had made it clear that she wouldn't allow it.

"You're older. You've had a wife," she'd said ominously. "Dorcas is an innocent young woman. Best you remain under the watchful eye of her parents and not risk falling to temptations of the flesh."

He found several flaws in Martha's line of thinking. First, Dorcas wasn't that young. No one had mentioned her exact age, and he wasn't about to ask, but he guessed that she was probably close to thirty. And the fact that he had reached an age of maturity meant that he was far *less* likely to behave inappropriately with a young woman than he had been in his youth. Furthermore, he and Dorcas weren't yet courting, and if he didn't get to know her, how could either of them know if they wanted to take the arrangement further?

Caleb kicked at the snow. He wanted to take this whole thing with Dorcas slowly, especially since it had started so suddenly. He hadn't intended to commit himself to visiting every Sunday and Wednesday, but with Reuben laid up with his broken leg, it naturally fell to him to be at the Coblentz farm more frequently. Then Martha had brought up Dorcas's availability and it had snowballed from there. Now everyone seemed to assume that he and Dorcas were courting. Roman had even remarked on their impending marriage during the lunch break today, and Caleb had to make his position clear.

"There's nothing definite yet between us," he'd explained to Roman and Eli. "We're just *considering* walking out together."

Roman had shook his head and Eli had laughed. "Not what Martha's telling the womenfolk," Roman said between bites of his liverwurst sandwich. "My Fannie talks about you two marrying like it's a done deal."

Eli had poured himself another cup of coffee from his Thermos. "Nothing wrong with Dorcas."

"I wouldn't be talking with her if there was," he'd defended. "Dorcas is a suitable prospect. Her being a member of our church makes it easier. If I picked a wife from another state, she'd be homesick for her family."

"Ya," Roman had agreed with a chuckle. "That's a fine reason for picking a bride. You don't have to go far to find her."

"Romantic," Eli added with a straight face.

"Marriage is a partnership," Caleb had defended. "For the family and—"

"Ya, ya." Roman snapped his fingers. "But a little spark between you never hurts."

Was there a spark between them? Caleb wondered as he reached the farmyard. Not so far. But maybe when she was a little more comfortable with him, Dorcas would have more to say. Not that she didn't talk; it was just that most of her sentences were prefaced by "Mam says." The thing was, he didn't want to hear what Martha thought. It was Dorcas he was considering as a wife and companion, not her mother.

Maybe he could invite her to his shop. Rebecca had been there several times, and she'd always been interested in what he was working on and his plans for increasing the business. Doubtless, Dorcas would be curious about his ability to support her and want to know exactly what he did. He didn't know how good her math skills were. If Dorcas was proficient in numbers and could learn to do his bookwork as Fannie did for Roman, it would free him to spend more time in the shop.

Caleb glanced ahead. In the darkness, golden lamplight glowed from the kitchen windows of his house. Rebecca would have the woodstove burning, the table set and supper waiting. He'd hitch up the horse and drive her home before eating. It was too cold for her to walk home, and he worried about her on the road at dusk— too many cars and trucks passing by.

As he approached the farmhouse, Fritzy barked and Rebecca threw open the back door. "Come in out of the cold. You're late," she said. Red-gold curls escaped her scarf to curl around her rosy face. A smudge of flour streaked her chin, and she looked as sweet as a frosted ginger cookie.

Don't go there, Caleb thought. Rebecca Yoder was all wrong for him, and it did no good to allow himself foolish yearnings. If he was a younger man… If fire hadn't marred his features… If he hadn't been called as a preacher, or she was a more serious girl, then maybe. He caught himself up sharply. "Maybe or might fill no corncribs," his uncle used to say. He was the man he was, and Rebecca was the way God made her. A smart man didn't plague his mind with something that could never be.

"Dat!" As Caleb entered the house, Amelia ran and threw herself into his arms. "Rebecca showed me how to make biscuit pigs!" she cried. "A mama pig and baby pigs with raisin eyes. And we baked them in the oven, and—and I'm going to eat them for supper. With butter on their snouts. You can have one."

Stepping into the kitchen, Caleb swung his daughter high until the top of her head nearly brushed the ceiling. She squealed with excitement. "I'll eat your baby pigs," he teased in a gruff voice. "I'll gobble them up, one by one."

"*Ne,* Dat." She giggled. "One baby pig. You get one. Rebecca gets one. And I eat the rest!"

"We'll eat when we get back. I'll take you home, Rebecca. It's too cold for you to walk. Roads may be slippery."

Rebecca pulled a cast-iron frying pan full of biscuits from the oven. "Grace is coming by to pick me up at six, if you don't mind me staying a little longer. Her boy's school was closed today, and he was with Johanna."

"It's no bother." He slipped off his wet shoes and hung his coat and hat on hooks in the utility room. Then he padded in his socks to the kitchen sink to wash his hands. Wonderful smells filled the kitchen and his stomach rumbled with anticipation. "You're welcome to share our supper," he said.

"*Ne.* Thank you just the same, but Johanna invited us to eat with her." Rebecca lifted the top of a Dutch oven, revealing a roasted chicken with stuffing. "I hope you like scalloped sweet potatoes and apples."

"And apple cobber," Amelia supplied. "I put in the cinn-a-min."

"Amelia did help make the cobbler." Rebecca dished out a plate for him and a smaller one for his daughter. "She's going to be a wonderful cook."

Caleb took his seat at the table. "Will you at least sit with us?" he asked.

Rebecca shook her head. "I'll just slip into the parlor and finish the letter I've been writing to *The Budget*." Her blue eyes sparkled with mischief in the lamplight. "Uncle Reuben would be disappointed if I didn't share the news about his accident. I'm mentioning the auction you've arranged to help with his medical expenses, too. Some may want to come from out of state to attend." She went back to the stove and returned with the biscuits. As Amelia had claimed, there were a number of small, misshapen objects that could have been pigs.

"Mine!" Amelia said, reaching for one. "My baby pigs."

"Careful," Rebecca warned. "The pan is still hot. Don't burn yourself."

Caleb glanced at Rebecca. "Whatever possessed you to teach her to make biscuits shaped like animals?" he asked. "Learning to bake is a useful skill for a girl, but pigs?"

Rebecca's mouth tightened. "She's a child, Caleb. Sometimes she simply has to have fun. Not everything is about work."

"She's growing fast. She can't get away with the nonsense she did as a baby." With a twinge, he realized he was echoing a remark he'd heard Martha make when Amelia had tipped over the sugar bowl trying to dip her finger in. "Her mother would expect her to be brought up proper," he said. "Especially since I'm a—"

"*Ya, ya.* A preacher. I know. You've made that clear to me." Rebecca set a pitcher of milk on the table beside Amelia's empty glass—set it down hard enough to make the silverware rattle together. Her blue eyes darkened. "And, just so you know, Caleb, my father was a bishop. And he's the one who taught me to make pig biscuits." With a sharp nod of her chin, she turned and bustled, stiff shouldered, out of the kitchen.

Caleb stared after her, confused. What had he said to set her off? Was she annoyed with him because he'd questioned the wisdom of her odd-shaped biscuits? His gaze fell on the leather case containing the carved bracket with the exaggerated pendant and disappointment settled over him like a wet coat. *I suppose she won't want to look at the piece now,* he thought, as some of the warmth seeped out of the room.

"Dat?" Amelia stared at him in bewilderment. "Don't you like my biscuits?"

"*Ya,* they are good biscuits. Remember, grace first, before we eat." Caleb bowed his head for a few moments and then nodded to Amelia and picked up his own fork. The chicken and stuffing had smelled so good, but now each bite tasted like sawdust in his mouth.

Thankfully, he didn't have to talk. Amelia couldn't remain silent long and soon began to chatter on about her day. Apparently, they had scrubbed the floors upstairs and polished the furniture. "Rebecca hung our laundry in the attic," she explained. "I helped."

"*Gut,*" he said absently. There was a large open space on the third floor with finished walls, but no furniture. He'd thought, when he'd bought the house, he could easily put several more bedrooms up there, if he ever had the need. Chimneys ran up on each end of the house, and when the stoves were in use, the attic was warm and dry. Why hadn't he thought of that instead of stringing clotheslines across his kitchen in bad weather?

"Rebecca says that—"

"Enough about Rebecca," he said. "Finish your supper."

"But—"

"Amelia."

Her face fell, and she sniffed.

Caleb stared at his plate. He hadn't meant to be harsh with her, but he'd heard quite enough about— A rap at the back door interrupted his thoughts. Thinking that must be Rebecca's sister come to pick her up, he rose from his chair to let her in.

He hadn't even heard Grace's car. He walked back through the utility room to let her in but to his surprise, he found not a Mennonite woman but three Amish men standing on his little back porch. Behind them, he saw a horse and buggy in the snowy yard.

"We've come to talk with you about an important matter, Preacher." The man extended his hand. "Ray Stutzman. Next district over."

"Ray." Caleb shook his hand and waved the visitors in. He recognized Thomas Troyer, a stout elder with a long white beard. "Thomas."

The three stomped the snow off their feet and removed their outer jackets and hats. "Samson Hershberger," Thomas said, indicating a big man of about forty, with dark hair and a full beard.

"Samson." Caleb exchanged handshakes with Thomas and Samson before showing them into the kitchen. Amelia slipped out of her chair and dashed out of the room. "Sit down," Caleb said, picking up the dinner plates to set them in the sink. "Coffee?"

"If it's no trouble." Thomas took a seat. "Sorry to bother you at suppertime, but the weather might get worse. We wanted to speak to you—"

"Tonight," Ray finished. "Samson and I are neighbors over on Rose Valley Road."

Rebecca appeared in the doorway, saw the visitors and immediately went to the cupboard for cups. "Thomas." She nodded a greeting to the other two before asking, "How is your wife, Samson? Doing well, I hope? And the new baby?"

"Both well," he said with a smile. "Heard you were cleaning for Preacher Caleb."

She poured coffee and served the men, quickly clearing away the last of the dinner and bringing sugar and milk and a tray of cookies. "I'll leave you to your business," she said and went back into the other room.

"Usually she doesn't stay this late," Caleb explained. "Her ride will be here any minute."

"She's half sister to John Hartman's wife, isn't she?"

Caleb nodded. He didn't want to be rude, but he was curious as to what urgent business he might have with these men from another church district so important as to bring them out on a snowy night. But these Amish were no different from those men he'd known in Idaho. No business could be contracted until small talk was out of the way. First, the weather, the price of hay and the scarcity of reasonable farm land had to be discussed, chewed over and commented on at length.

Finally, just when Caleb had nearly lost patience and was ready to come right out and ask why they were there, Thomas got to the point. "What do you know about the Reapers?" he asked.

"Reapers?" Caleb had no idea what he was talking about.

"You know about the Gleaners," Samson said. "The young people's church group?"

"Of course." One of his jobs was to meet with them twice a month and approve projects, frolics and community outreach. "Charley Byler and his wife are the sponsors. Surely, the Gleaners haven't done anything—"

"Ne," Thomas replied. "The Gleaners have always been a responsible group. We find no fault with them. It's this new group, the Reapers."

"Teenagers from three of our local districts gathering. Yours included. I've had a report from the Delaware State Police of underage drinking of alcohol," Samson said. "Boys are sneaking out at night and attending parties with Englishers. The policemen told me that they broke up a bonfire in a field near Black Bottom. They caught some of the English kids, but the Amish boys ran into the woods."

"There's no *Rumspringa* in Kent County," Ray said. "We don't allow it. Too dangerous. We need your support to settle this behavior before someone is hurt."

"I agree, but why come to me?" Caleb asked. "I have only the one child, and you saw her. She's not even old enough for school."

"We would have asked Reuben for help." Samson leaned forward on his elbows on the table. He wore long johns under his shirt, and the wrists were worn thin from wear. "He's been successful with wayward teenagers before, but Reuben's laid up with that broken leg. You're the other preacher for Seven Poplars. We were hoping you'd step in."

Caleb rose to pour another cup of coffee. His was still half full, but he needed the excuse to gather his thoughts. Bad enough that he'd been thrust into the position of preacher to his own district, a job he doubted he was up to. But this? If he failed to influence the boys and change their dangerous behavior, he'd disappoint his congregation and maybe shame their district in front of the others. "I'm not sure I'm the right man for this," he said hesitantly.

"I'd do it myself, but I'm too old," Thomas said. "The teens feel no connection to most of our elders. And Samson, here, he—"

"My boy Joe is one of the ringleaders of this bunch," Samson admitted. "I've tried talking to him, tried punishment, but Joe is eighteen and feeling his oats. It would break his mother's heart if he was arrested or got hurt in this nonsense."

Caleb looked at Ray. "You, Ray?"

Ray shook his head. "I was pretty wild when I was their age, and they all know it. My Paul said as much to me. He said they weren't doing anything wrong, but they are. The world is a temptation our kids aren't equipped to face. First it will be drugs, then who knows what? You've heard what goes on in Kansas with some of the young people? Drinking alcohol and worse."

Caleb nodded. "I have, and it troubles me. To think that children raised in the faith could stray so far."

"Amen to that," Ray agreed. "It's why we've come, why we ask you to meet with these kids, try to convince them that they are on the path to real trouble."

"You say some of our teenagers are involved?" Caleb asked. "Do you have names to give me?"

"Only three I know for sure," Thomas answered. "Vernon and Elmer Beachy and their cousin, Irwin Beachy. He lives with the schoolteacher, Hannah Yoder."

Chapter Twelve

"Irwin?" Rebecca said to Caleb. "I've heard rumors about these Reapers, but I had no idea that Irwin was involved. Mam will have him cleaning the stables until he's twenty-one!" It was all Rebecca had been able to do to remain out of sight in the parlor until the visitors were gone. But she'd heard every word the men exchanged.

"It's a bad business." Caleb glanced in the direction of the parlor.

"It's all right," Rebecca assured him, knowing he was concerned Amelia might overhear them. "She's playing with her doll on the rug near the fireplace where it's warm." The parlor and that section of the house were heated with a new pellet stove that stood on a tile platform in a fireplace. There was a child-protection screen to keep Amelia from falling against it and getting burned.

Caleb glanced up at the clock and then out the window. "Grace is late."

"I know." Snow was still falling, but there was no wind, and it didn't appear to Rebecca that a storm was brewing. "She's usually on time. Something must have delayed her." She began to take the dirty coffee mugs to the sink.

"Leave them," Caleb said, taking a seat at the kitchen table. "I can do that later."

She slipped into the chair across from him. "So, what are you going to do about the boys? It *is* just boys, isn't it? They didn't say any of our girls were involved, did they?"

Caleb's brow furrowed and he rubbed his fingertips along his scarred cheek. "*Ne,* no Amish girls, but some English. Maybe Charley would have some ideas of what to say to our kids."

She thought for a moment before she spoke. "You know I love Charley. He's been like a brother to me since he and Miriam married, but I'd trust your judgment before I would his—on something like this. Charley is…" She sought the right word. "Innocent. He's really like a big kid himself. I think you're a better choice in this situation. You'll find a way to guide these boys back to the right path."

Caleb folded his arms and looked at her. "You think I'm up to it?"

"I know you are," she answered.

He nodded. For once, the rigid mask slipped, and Rebecca could see the man behind it: the Caleb who wasn't bearing the weight of the world on his shoulders. "It's good you think so," he said. "I have doubts about myself, doubts about being chosen as a preacher for our church. I failed my family once, when it mattered, and I guess I'm always afraid that…"

"You didn't fail." She extended her hand across the table, and Caleb's lean, scarred fingers closed around hers. What was strange was that she barely felt the scars.

Instead, she felt the strength. "What happened with your wife. You tried to save her, but bad things happen sometimes." She pressed her lips together. "I think trying to do the right thing now is what God wants of us."

He squeezed her hand and then released it, leaving her with a sense of loss. She could still feel the power and the warmth of his grip, and she wanted it again. "Caleb…"

Once, when she was small, when the family was just getting ready for dinner, Mam had asked her to keep an eye on Susanna. But she and her sisters were playing tag, and she forgot. When she remembered to look for Susanna, she found that she'd chased a duck out onto the frozen pond. Only, it was March, and the ice wasn't solid.

Ruth had run for Dat, but Rebecca had been afraid that the ice would crack and Susanna would fall in and drown. Instead of getting a clothes pole like Ruth had told her, she'd crept out on the pond. By the time she got to Susanna, ice had splintered under her weight in long thin cracks like spiderwebs.

Rebecca had been terrified, trying not to cry, and all the while, Susanna was laughing and pointing at the pretty patterns in the ice. Rebecca had gotten hold of her sister's hand and together they had crawled, inch by inch, back toward the bank.

"Stay where you are!" Leah had screamed. "Wait for Dat! Stay there!"

But, some inner voice had warned her that she had to keep moving. If they stopped, they'd sink into that deep, cold water. They'd reached solid land safely, but she had never forgotten the terrifying sensation of ice bending beneath her feet. She felt like that now, with

Caleb, afraid to remain where she was and terrified to move forward.

"I *know* you can do this," she told him firmly.

He stood and began to pace the linoleum floor. "It seems you have more faith in me than I do." He paused near the doorway and glanced back at her. "How does a young woman gain so much confidence about a man she hardly knows?"

She leaned forward. "You weren't the only one surprised when you were chosen as our new preacher. Everyone was. You were new to Seven Poplars. No one really knew what you were like. And you were a widower who hadn't remarried. I've never heard of a preacher who didn't have a wife when he was called."

"And?"

"I'm just a woman, but I try to follow the teachings of the church. I read my Bible and I pray every day, but I'm not wise. All I know is that God chose you. And if He believes in you, Caleb, why shouldn't I?"

A smiled softened the curves of his lips. "It sounds so simple when you say it, Rebecca. Sensible." He chuckled. "I hope you're right—"

The sound of a car horn outside brought Rebecca to her feet. "That must be Grace." She reached for her cloak and the heavy mittens Mam had insisted she wear when she walked over this morning. "It will be all right," she told him.

He held her gaze for a long moment, then turned away. "Amelia! Rebecca's leaving. Come say good night."

"I'll see you tomorrow." Rebecca's feet felt heavy. She didn't want to leave, but she knew she had to. Her hand still tingled where Caleb had touched her and her chest felt tight. Was this what it felt like to love a man? *Love?* She shivered, but it was a shiver of excitement, not fear. She knew that it was too late to go back. Coming here, being part of Caleb and Amelia's household had become more than a job.

Amelia came running for a hug and Rebecca bent to embrace her.

"Thank you," Caleb said.

"I didn't do anything," she answered breathlessly as they walked to the back door and she opened it.

"You did," he insisted, swinging Amelia up into his arms. He opened the back door for Rebecca. "More than you'll ever know. I just want you to know I appreciate it."

The driver's door opened and Grace stepped out of the SUV. "Sorry," she called. "I was held up on Route 1. A chicken truck jackknifed and both lanes were closed. There were chickens everywhere."

"How terrible." Rebecca hurried out of the house, closing the door behind her, putting distance between her and Caleb. "Was anyone injured?"

Grace shook her head. "I don't think so. It was just the truck, no other vehicles. It must have been the slippery road."

Big snowflakes coated the SUV, the ground, the house and buildings and Grace's mane of curly red hair, covered only by a tiny lace prayer cap. Rebecca hugged her.

Grace was dressed in a jean skirt, a sweater topped by a leather coat and boots to her knees. "Johanna will have our heads for delaying her supper," she said. "I hope she hasn't worried."

Rebecca went around to the passenger's door and

got in. The heater was running, and the automobile was toasty warm. "Wait until you hear what I just found out about Irwin," she said. "He is in so much in trouble."

"He's not the only one." Grace pointed. "At the crossroads, I had to slam on my brakes and swerve to keep from hitting that old buggy that Elmer Beachy's been driving—the one decked out in red-and-green Christmas lights."

"What?" Rebecca stared at her. "Are you sure it was Elmer?"

"Certain. He had a bunch of other boys in there with him. Some of them were hanging out the back door, yelling and waving, acting stupid. I wondered what Lydia was thinking, letting them take a horse and buggy out on a night like this."

"What direction were they going?"

"They turned on to Thompson's dirt lane, the one that runs along the edge of his property line. I don't know where they were going. It's not likely the kids would be having a bonfire tonight, in this weather, is it?"

"Did you see Irwin with them?"

Grace shook her head as she turned the key in the ignition. "No, but I wouldn't have recognized Elmer if it wasn't for the Christmas lights and his horse. It was a paint. Almost every Amish man in this county drives a bay. Elmer's horse is brown and white. Plus he was wearing that beat-up cowboy hat of his." She put the SUV in Reverse. "I talked to John. He swung by and picked up 'Kota after work, so if Johanna's invitation is still open—"

"Stop!" Rebecca exclaimed. "Stop the car."

Grace applied the brakes. "What's wrong?" She squinted. "Chickens in the driveway?"

"*Ne,* worse. A lot worse." Rebecca unfastened her seat belt. "There's something Caleb and I have to do right away. Can you take Amelia to Johanna's?"

"Sure, but why?"

"I'll explain later," she said getting out of the car. "But if those Beachy boys are up to no good and Irwin is with them, I've got to try to stop it."

"How much trouble could they cause on a private dirt road?"

"You'd be surprised."

"I can't believe I let you talk me into this," Caleb said. "How are we ever going to find that buggy? It's been a good twenty minutes since Grace saw the boys at the crossroads." He slapped the reins over his horse's back and guided the animal down the blacktop.

There were few cars and trucks on the road. It was still snowing, and Rebecca hadn't seen a single Amish person since they'd left Caleb's house. She sat up straight on the cushioned buggy seat, very conscious of Caleb only inches away. Being unchaperoned with him on a woods road at night was definitely stretching the rules, but the members of the Seven Poplars church district were sensible. If she and Caleb could show they'd been on an errand of supervision—keeping Amish kids out of trouble—the breach would be forgiven.

"We might be able to catch up with them if they took the Thompson lane," she explained. The Thompsons were Englishers. "They may not know that there's a new gate on the far side of the woods. The owners just put it up this week. Mam heard at Spence's that Thompson's nephew had reported someone breaking into his uncle's abandoned farmhouse. The police advised him to put up a locked gate to keep people from driving back to the farm. They rent out the land to a farmer, but no one has lived in the house for twenty years. It doesn't even have electricity anymore."

"What makes you think Elmer Beachy and our boys would break into that house?" The lazy, fat snowflakes had given way to smaller flakes that were now coming down as if they had no intention of stopping until the snow lay six inches deep. The temperature had dropped in the past hour, and Rebecca was glad of the thick wool blanket that Caleb had brought from the house and insisted that she tuck around her lap and legs.

"You're new to Kent County, so there's no way you'd know. About five years ago, some English teenagers were using the farmhouse as a place to hold parties. They got pretty wild and even started a fire in the fireplace. Some parents caught on and called the authorities before someone was hurt or the house burned down. So it wouldn't surprise me if the same kids who were now having bonfire parties decided to use the old Thompson place. There are no neighbors, and the house is in the deep woods and has a really long lane. No one would hear them back there."

"You better be right, Rebecca. If you're wrong, I've sent my daughter to your sister's house to spend the night and compromised both our reputations to take a long, cold buggy ride in the snow."

"I'm afraid I am right. Think about it. Isn't it suspicious that the Beachy brothers are out on such a bad night? There isn't a singing, and neither of them are old enough to be walking out with girls." She paused long enough to draw in a quick breath and went on. "Besides, Grace said there was a buggy full of boys. Mam was just saying that Irwin was going to bed awfully early lately, but he still looks red eyed and tired in the morning. She was going to buy him some vitamins."

"So he could be sneaking out with his cousins?"

"Turn here." Rebecca pointed to an opening in a grove of cedar trees. "It's an old logging road and it can get muddy in wet weather, but the ground will be frozen solid tonight."

Caleb guided the horse off the paved road. "I don't see any tracks, Amish or English."

Rebecca shook her head. "Trust me, Caleb. I grew up here. There's a tangle of lanes and dirt roads that run for miles through woodland and back pastures. My sisters and I used to ride ponies back here when we were young, and before that, we went cutting wood and looking for wild bees with my *dat.* Most of the trails are grown over, but we can still squeeze through." She spoke with more confidence than she felt. "If they're headed for the Thompson house, we can still get there ahead of them."

The lane had deep ruts, and they couldn't see more than a few yards ahead of the horse, but once they were sheltered by the old growth forest, it was easier driving. Ten minutes stretched like thirty, and Rebecca was beginning to fear that she'd made a terrible mistake when the horse snorted and perked up its ears.

"Listen," Rebecca said. "Do you hear that?"

Caleb reined in the horse. Without the soft thud of the animal's hooves and the creak of the buggy, Rebecca could clearly hear music up ahead. Loud, thumping music!

"Not hymns, for certain," Caleb remarked.

"Hurry," she urged. "This lane meets up with another one just beyond the trees. The house will be on the left in a clearing, and our kids should be driving from the right."

Caleb slapped the reins over the horse's rump, and the buggy lurched ahead. Rebecca's stomach rose in her throat, and she clutched the dashboard of the carriage.

The level of noise rose, and when they broke out of the woods, Rebecca wasn't surprised to hear the blare of a car horn and shrieks of laughter. Pickup trucks, SUVs and automobiles crowded the open space around the house and lined the dirt road on either side. Lights bobbed behind shuttered windows, and someone had built a huge fire of fence posts and logs near the front door—much too near the house for safety. English boys and girls ran across the clearing, whooping and shouting. Most seemed to be drinking out of cans, but Rebecca couldn't tell if they had soft drinks or something more inappropriate. As she stared, she heard the crack of glass and wood and saw something pitch through an upstairs window, followed by peals of shrill laughter.

"This is bad," Caleb said. "Do you see any buggies?"

"*Ne,* but it's so dark…." She scanned the area around the fire. From their clothes, most of the kids seemed to be Englishers, but she couldn't be sure. Amish kids were known to leave their house in their own homemade clothing and change into Englisher clothes on the way to this sort of thing. "What do we do?" she asked Caleb. "If our kids are here, we can't leave them."

"*We* will do nothing. You'll stay here and I'll go and see for myself," he answered. "Don't get out of the buggy. I'll turn the horse around first, so if...if anything frightens you, just drive back the way we came."

"I couldn't leave you," she insisted.

"*Ne,* Rebecca." His voice was firm. "I'm capable of looking after myself. If I'm not back in five minutes, you—"

"Look!" She caught his arm. "Coming up the lane. See!"

In the distance, she could see telltale blinking red-and-green Christmas lights. "Elmer's buggy. We got here ahead of them."

"*Ya,*" Caleb agreed. "Looks as though you were right. But what about that gate you mentioned? The one that was supposed to be locked?"

"With all these cars and trucks here, the English kids must have broken through. We can go out that way." She pointed left. "It's a good mile shorter to the main road."

"A mile? How's that possible?"

"The Thompson farm isn't on the hardtop. There's a right-of-way drive through Joe King's farm." She shivered as a clump of snow from an overhanging branch fell onto the dashboard and splattered over her.

"Walk on," Caleb said to the horse. "We've come this far. Best finish this mess as quick as we can." He glanced at her. She couldn't see the expression in his eyes, but she was certain that there was a hint of amusement in his voice.

She smiled in surprise. "You're enjoying this, aren't you?"

"Am not," he said brusquely.

Rebecca stifled a chuckle. Who would have thought that Caleb had a sense of adventure? "Now all you have to do is convince the Beachy boys and whoever else is with them to go home."

"Oh, they'll go home, all right," he assured her. "One way or another, they're going home." Caleb urged his horse faster, cutting off the approaching buggy a good fifty yards from the house and bonfire. "Stay where you are," he said as pulled up and jumped down from the seat.

A moment later, Rebecca heard Caleb's voice and the subdued ones of the boys, but try as she could, she was unable to hear exactly what was being said. She was tempted to get out and walk over, despite Caleb's warning her not to. But before she could get up the nerve, he came striding back, climbed up and turned his horse.

"Are they coming with us?" she ventured.

"What do you think?"

"Was Irwin with them?"

"Irwin, the two Beachy boys and two others. I don't know their names, but they're Amish."

"They haven't been drinking, have they?"

"*Ne.* Although I think those Englishers are. The boys have no alcohol or tobacco in the buggy."

"Good." A sense of relief swept over her. "What will you do? Will you go to their parents?"

"I will. I'd not try to keep this night's mischief to myself. But I told the boys I'd be meeting with them to discuss the matter further and that there would be consequences from the church."

"What will you say to them?"

Caleb sighed. "I'll pray on it, Rebecca. God sent you to show me the way tonight. I have no doubt that He won't abandon me when I talk with the boys later." He laid his hand over hers and she shivered again. This time, it wasn't from the cold. "I hope you don't mind. I'm going to take these boys home in the Beachy buggy. I'll follow you to your mother's, then be on my way. I told Irwin to come up and ride home with you. I'll come back for my buggy at your mother's place in the morning. The Beachy boys can come for their buggy when their parents see fit."

"Whatever you say, Caleb." She felt a twinge of disappointment that she wouldn't be riding home with him. She heard the shuffle of feet and saw a crestfallen Irwin appear at the side of the buggy. "Will you drive, or shall I?" she asked him.

"You best drive, Rebecca. Irwin hasn't shown the best of judgment tonight. I'm not sure I want to trust him with your safety."

Gathering the reins in her hands, she clicked to the horse. There wasn't a sound from Irwin as she headed for home. Soon, the house and the noisy party were behind them and only the snowy lane lay ahead.

"I'm sorry," Irwin began. "I didn't…"

"Save it for Mam," she said. "I'm too disappointed with you to talk about this tonight."

They were almost to the main road when Rebecca heard sirens and saw the flash of lights. Her heart raced and then sunk as a Delaware State police car turned off the blacktop and came directly toward her. Shaking, she reined the horse off the center of the lane to allow them to pass.

They didn't. The lead vehicle came to a stop beside her, and two state troopers got out. One shone a light into her face and looked at her for a moment. "Sorry to bother you, ma'am," he said. "We're investigating a report of trespassing and underage drinking. Where are you headed?"

"Home, with my brother."

"You be careful, then," the trooper instructed.

She nodded. "Have a good evening." Then she lifted the reins and urged the horse forward.

When she looked back, however, she saw that Caleb, driving the Beachy buggy with the garish red-and-green flashing Christmas lights, hadn't been so fortunate. The police had stopped him as well, but had not waved them on. Caleb and his passengers were climbing down onto the snowy lane, their pale faces illuminated by a glaring spotlight.

Chapter Thirteen

The following morning was cold and still, and a crust of snow crunched under the buggy wheels as Caleb drove the Beachy buggy up into the Yoder barnyard. He'd disconnected the battery so that the ridiculous red-and-green lights no longer blinked, something he wished he'd taken the time to do when he'd climbed up onto the bench seat the night before.

He'd taken down the big foam dice and removed the speakers for the boom box, but there was nothing he could do to hide the florescent orange triangles painted on each side of the carriage. Every Amish vehicle that was driven on the road had to have a large orange reflector on the back to satisfy Delaware traffic laws, but in Caleb's opinion the Beachy boys had gone overboard with their nonsense. He felt more conspicuous driving this hot-rod buggy in the daytime than he did at night.

A single set of fresh footprints crossed the yard from the back door of the house to the barn. The tracks were small and neat, definitely not left by Irwin's size-eleven muck boots. Anticipation made Caleb sit up a little straighter on the bench seat. He hoped the early riser might be Rebecca and not Hannah or Susanna. As part of the evening's escapade, Rebecca would be the last person to poke fun at him for being seen in the outrageous buggy.

He reined in the horse and swung down out of the seat. He'd turn the animal in to a box stall in the stable. Elmer could come for his horse later today. Caleb had dropped off the two brothers last night before taking the other two boys home, but he wasn't doing them any more favors by returning the horse and buggy. They could walk over to retrieve it, providing their father ever let them leave the house again. As it was, they'd gotten off easy. They hadn't been arrested and hadn't caused the community public shame—perhaps even unwanted pictures in the Dover newspaper. That would have been hard to live down.

Caleb unharnessed the horse and walked it to the barn, still deep in thought.

Immediate disaster had been avoided by getting the boys away from the party before the police arrived, but preventing future indiscretions would be more difficult. Caleb knew that teenage boys had short memories. The talking-to he'd given the miscreants the previous night was only the first step in changing their behavior. He had spent an hour on his knees this morning praying that God would give him the wisdom to live up to the task.

As Caleb entered the Yoder barn, he looked up to see Rebecca coming down the ladder from the hayloft. For a few seconds, he didn't call out to her. She was such a pretty sight, all pink cheeked from the cold, red curls tumbling around her face and small graceful hands—

hands that could bake bread, soothe a crying child and manage a spirited driving horse without hesitation.

"Caleb!" A smile lit her eyes and spread over her face. "I didn't expect you so early."

"Ya." Why did he always sound as though he was about to deliver a sermon when he spoke to her? Most times, he felt at ease around people he knew, but Rebecca often made him trip over his own tongue. "You too," he added. "Up early."

She nodded. "I like mornings, when it's quiet. And when there's snow or rain, it seems even quieter. A barn can be almost like a church. Don't you think so? The contented sounds of the animals, the rustle of hay when you throw it down from the loft." She laughed softly. " must sound foolish."

"Ne. I feel the same way. Not so much like when the bishop gives a sermon, but as if…as if God is listening."

"Exactly." She came down the last few rungs to the floor, folded her arms and stood there, smiling at him almost as if she was waiting for something.

He cleared his throat. "Your mother? Did she ask what happened? Was she angry that you got home so late?"

"Not angry." The corners of Rebecca's eyes crinkled as her mood became more serious. "Concerned. But when I explained what we did, why we had to go and fetch Irwin and the others home, she understood." Rebecca arched an eyebrow. "She was very unhappy with Irwin, and she let him know it."

Caleb led the horse into a stall, backed out and closed the gate. "Will she punish him?"

Rebecca brushed hay off her skirt. "Mam has always been good at finding the right punishment for each o her children, and her pupils. I think she'll find extra work for him to do. He won't have so much free time to think up mischief." She went to a feed bin, lifted the wooden lid and scooped out a measure of grain.

"That's what I was thinking." Caleb walked over to stand nearer, and he caught a whiff of green apples. The scent was one he'd come to associate with Rebecca, and he supposed it must be her shampoo. Hannah was sometimes lenient with her daughters, but wouldn't allow Rebecca to wear perfume. Green apple was a plain smell, clean and honest. He liked it, maybe more than he wanted to admit. "What I thought would be best," he said.

She looked at him expectantly.

"I know the parents will want to reprimand their sons as they see fit, but I think that there should be something more." He swallowed, suddenly nervous that Rebecca wouldn't agree his plan was the wisest—that she might think he was too lenient. "That's to say, if the elders and the parents think that it's a good idea, I want to meet with the boys every Saturday. Not for punishment, but for counseling."

Rebecca's blue eyes sparked with interest, and he went on with more confidence. When she looked at him, he got the feeling she saw beyond the scars on his face and hand. It was almost as if she didn't see them at all. "I want each boy to take responsibility for another person or couple—elderly, or those with health problems. And not from the church district they belong to. That would be too easy. They should already be caring for their own grandparents, their own neighbors. I want them to help someone in another district. And not just for a few weeks. I want them to paint, repair, fetch and carry, do whatever's needed for a full year." He waited, unconsciously holding his breath for her reaction.

"Caleb, that's a wonderful idea," she pronounced. Understanding flooded her animated features, and her gaze grew warm. "A year of helping someone who needs it. That could make a difference, not just for the teens but for those receiving the help. You could change lives in a year."

"I hope so." He felt the tenseness drain from his shoulders. "These are good boys, just…"

"Just kids," she said. "It's not easy to grow up. But…" She fiddled with one of the ties that hung from her *kapp*.

"But what?"

"I wonder…"

"*Ya?* A suggestion?"

She nodded. "I think they need fun, too, a little excitement. Nothing the elders wouldn't approve of, but perhaps…" Now she looked at him hesitantly. "Maybe you could take them places like to a baseball game or a camping trip to a national park? Interesting places that they've never seen."

"Show them some of the English world?"

"*Ya,* Caleb. Let them see that ours is a good place, but that it isn't wrong to want to see elephants and eat cotton candy and watch trains."

"Trains?" He nodded, trying to hide a surge of excitement. As a boy, he'd been fascinated by trains, but he'd never gotten to ride on one. "They would like that, to ride on one, you think?"

"I'm sure they would. I know I would. You could take them on Amtrak to a work frolic in an Amish community in another state. It could be a reward for completing their year of service."

He grinned at her. "A reward for doing right. I like that idea, Rebecca. I like it a lot, and if we were going for a reason—say to help raise a barn or dig a well in another Amish community, I think the elders would approve." He chuckled. "And I would like the train ride, too."

"Caleb." He turned to see Rebecca's mother standing in the doorway. "I saw the horse and buggy." Hannah smiled at him, but Caleb sensed that she wasn't entirely comfortable to find him alone in the barn with her Rebecca.

"I was just about to ask Rebecca if she thought it was too early for me to pick up Amelia at Johanna's," he said.

"I can do that for you," Rebecca offered. She hurried to the nearest box stall and dumped a scoop of grain into the feed box. Blackie pushed his nose into the fragrant horse chow. "There's no sense in you being late for work. We can drive back to the chair shop and then I can go and get Amelia. I'd like to go to Byler's this morning, anyway. You need groceries."

"That will work out fine," he agreed. "It was kind of your sister to keep Amelia overnight. We don't want to wear out her welcome."

"Not to worry about that," Hannah assured him. "Katy loves Amelia, and her having someone to play with makes Johanna's life easier. Katy can be as full of mischief as her brother if she isn't kept busy." Hannah tilted her head. "There's just one thing I want to know."

"Ya?"

"When the policemen stopped you last night? What did you say to them?"

He glanced at Rebecca.

"I told Mam how scared I was when they made you get out of the buggy," she explained.

"I was pretty scared myself," Caleb admitted. "I just told the police that I was following you home, to see that you got home safe on such a snowy night."

Hannah chuckled. "That was the truth, I suppose. You *were* following Rebecca." She looked back at him. "And they didn't ask why you had so many boys with you?"

Caleb shook his head. "They looked them over to see if they'd been drinking and waved us back into the buggy. I couldn't lie, but the police didn't ask where the boys had been headed, and I didn't offer."

Hannah crossed her arms over her chest and studied Caleb for a moment. "I like you, Caleb. You're a man who knows when to speak and when not to." She gave him a smile and walked away.

Rebecca looked at Caleb. He looked at her, and they both laughed; for just a moment, Rebecca found herself lost in his merry brown eyes.

Sunday was a visiting day, and Mam had invited Grossmama, Aunt Martha, Uncle Reuben, Dorcas, Bishop Atlee, Aunt Jezzy and her husband, Nip, and Caleb and Amelia to dinner. Even though Ruth had come over the previous day to help with the salads, pies and ham, there were still a few things to do. The bishop's wife had gone to stay with a daughter who was expecting a baby, so the church members were taking turns having the bishop over for meals.

The truth was, Rebecca hadn't really wanted any company today. Although she usually loved visiting Sundays, today she was restless. It seemed as if she hadn't had a moment to herself all week, and since the night she and Caleb had gone to round up the boys, she needed time to think.

She liked Caleb—more than liked him—and she was beginning to realize that her interest went beyond respect and friendship. The previous weekend, she'd seen another side of him, and they'd shared a real adventure. Caleb had shown that he was willing to risk his reputation and bend the rules for a greater good. And then, the following morning, when he'd shared his plans and seemed genuinely interested in her opinion, she'd suspected that the weak feeling in her knees and the quickening heartbeat and giddiness she'd felt went beyond a parishioner's approval of her preacher. She realized she was falling in love with him.

No, she corrected herself sternly, not falling—had fallen in love with him. It had already happened, sometime in the days and weeks since she'd begun caring for Amelia and his house. Every instinct told her that Caleb felt the same about her. Of course, he hadn't said so in words. And certainly not his actions. Worse, everyone said he was courting Dorcas.

Rebecca felt so confused. Maybe he hadn't been completely honest with her; maybe Caleb really was walking out with her cousin. Grossmama believed it. Aunt Jezzy and all the neighbors already saw Caleb and Dorcas as a couple. And over the past few weeks, Aunt Martha had certainly told everyone who would listen what a fine match the new preacher would be for her daughter. Only Caleb continued to insist that he and Dorcas were spending time with each other to see if they wanted to court.

So Rebecca was in a quandary. What did she do

about these feelings for Caleb? It wasn't her place to initiate a conversation with him concerning their possible mutual feelings. Amish men were the ones responsible for starting such talk. Rebecca knew she could be bold at times, but she didn't think this was a time when she could step beyond the customs of her community. What if she was wrong, and Caleb really did care for Dorcas and not her? She'd embarrass herself and Caleb.

"Becca." Susanna tugged on her apron. "Becca. You're not listening." She was persistent and now was tugging at her sleeve. "Becca, Mam is mean," she said.

"What?" Rebecca sank down on the top step of the staircase. She'd been on her way upstairs to get a clean apron from her bedroom when she'd gotten sidetracked by her introspection. The sight of Susanna's tearstained face made her instantly ashamed. "What's wrong, Susanna banana?"

"I want King David to eat, too. Mam said, 'Not today.' But I *want* him to come. Not fair."

"David was here for breakfast just yesterday," Rebecca reminded her. She dug in her apron pocket for a tissue and handed it to her sister. "Blow."

Susanna did as she was told, blowing so hard that her eyes watered. "I want King David," she repeated. "Mam is mean if he can't…can't come." She thrust out her lower lip in a pout. "She wants to keep me and him…" Susanna's forehead creased with concentration as she searched for the right word. "Not together!" She sniffed and wiped at the end of her nose. "Mam hates him."

"Ne." Rebecca slipped an arm around Susanna's trembling shoulders. "Mam doesn't hate anyone, and she certainly doesn't hate David. She likes him."

Susanna looked up hopefully. "She does? He can come eat ham?"

Rebecca shook her head. "Not today. Another day. You can't see each other every day. It isn't proper. You aren't children. If you spend too much time together, people will talk."

"But…but King David and me…we're walking out. I'm going to marry him."

"Susanna. Hush, don't say such things. You aren't going to marry David. You can't."

Susanna's round blue eyes narrowed. "You're mean, too. You don't believe me. I love him."

Rebecca caught Susanna's chin in her hand and tenderly tilted it up. She wondered if this was a problem Mam ever thought she'd have to address with Susanna. Like Rebecca and all of her sisters, had she assumed Susanna would never have the inclination to marry? "It's complicated, sister. It's like we all have our jobs to do. You can't get married. You have to stay home and take care of Mam."

"Ne." Susanna shook her head so hard that her cap slipped sideways. "You think I'm stupid. I'm not stupid. I can peel apples and marry King David if I want." Rising to her feet, she pulled away and ran down the stairs, nearly colliding with their mother at the foot of the steps before veering off toward the kitchen.

"What's wrong with Susanna?" Mam said, coming up.

Susanna was already out of sight.

"She's upset that David can't come to dinner today," Rebecca explained. "I tried to—"

"I know," her mother answered. "Come with me. I was looking for you, and I wanted to talk to you about something." She pulled an envelope out of her pocket. "I got this from Leah yesterday."

"Is something wrong?"

"*Ne.* Nothing like that." Mam shook her head. "We should talk in your room."

Rebecca followed her into her bedroom and watched, puzzled, as her mother closed the door. Having her sister far away at a jungle mission in Brazil was worrisome. Leah was the sister she'd been closest to in age. They had gone together to care for Grossmama in Ohio before moving her to Delaware. Rebecca and Leah had never been apart until Leah's marriage.

"Your sister says that Daniel's aunt Joyce and her husband have been called to spend three months at a Mennonite orphanage a few hundred miles from the mission where she and Daniel live. They've booked passage on a container ship and they'll be going right after Christmas. They'll be taking a few truckloads of blankets, clothes, shoes and medical supplies to the orphanage, but they have room for two more passengers. Leah wants you and Susanna to come stay with her for the three months. She's says she's been lonesome for the sight of family, that she wants you to come, and I think you should."

"But Miriam and Charley—"

"Are already there. Yes, I know. But they can't stay long. Charley needs to get back to work. If you girls went, you'd go with Daniel's family and then return with them three months later."

"Susanna and I?" Rebecca caught hold of the end of the iron bed. "Go to Brazil?"

"You could be with your sister. Leah will be thrilled to have you and..." Mam's voice trailed off.

"And?" Rebecca looked at her suspiciously.

Mam nodded. "And I think it would be a good thing to get Susanna away from David King for a time. I know what she's been upset about for the past few months. She has this notion in her head that they're going to be married and I've tried to make her understand that's not going to happen."

"I tried to tell her, too." Rebecca met her mother's gaze and held it. "But is it Susanna you want to send away, or is it me?"

Chapter Fourteen

Her mother reached for her hand, and instantly Rebecca felt a twinge of remorse for the sharpness of her retort. "I'm sorry," Rebecca murmured. "I didn't mean to be rude. It's just that Ruth keeps bringing up Caleb, and even Anna and Miriam think—"

"That you had set your *kapp* for him?" Hannah's fingers closed around Rebecca's. "That you would like to have Caleb for yourself, even though he's courting your cousin?"

"He *isn't* courting her," Rebecca protested, pulling her hand free. She sat on the bed, slipped out of her shoes and tucked her feet up under her skirt. "Caleb says that they're getting to know each other, to see *if*—"

"I don't know how they do things in Idaho, but Dorcas thinks they're walking out." Mam frowned. "She told Charley's sister Mary that her mother wanted them to announce the banns soon so that they could marry in the spring." She hesitated. "Is there something going on I should know about?"

"*Ne.* Of course not." A heaviness settled on Rebecca.

"But I won't lie to you. I...I could have feelings for him."

Her mother sat beside her on the bed. "Has he told you that his affection for you goes further than friendship? That he looks on you as more than someone to clean his house and care for his child?"

Rebecca looked away. "Not in so many words." The heaviness had become a lump in the pit of her stomach. Maybe it was just her imagination that Caleb liked her. She looked back at her mother hesitantly. "You think I should go to Leah in Brazil?"

"I think it would be wise. Without you here in Seven Poplars," Hannah continued, "Caleb will make his intentions clear to Dorcas. If the two of them part ways after you leave, no one can say you ruined your cousin's chance at a good marriage." Mam's mouth tightened. "This may be Dorcas's only opportunity. She's my niece and I love her, but she's often at a loss as to how to show her good heart."

"Which is a nice way of saying Dorcas can be prickly."

Hannah smiled. "Some people find it more difficult to understand others. And Martha hasn't always been the best example. I don't mean to be critical, but if Dorcas would think before she speaks, I believe she would have more friends."

Rebecca gripped her mother's hand, feeling lost and confused. "You know I wouldn't want to hurt Dorcas." Thoughts of never seeing Caleb come home, of not sharing jokes and the day's events with him made her sad. "But if I leave, what will happen to Amelia?"

"I've already thought of that. Johanna will watch her during the day. We already discussed it." Mam sighed.

"And by the time you come home, you might feel differently about Caleb."

"And if I don't?"

"Then he will either be your cousin by marriage or the two of you will have a chance to start fresh—to court openly." Mam was quiet for a minute. "Whether you go or not, I think it may be time to make other arrangements for Amelia's care. I don't think it's wise for you to work for him anymore. You're thrown together too often. If he wasn't our preacher, it never would have been permitted. But even the faithful can be tempted into dangerous behavior."

"You really want Susanna and me to go?"

Her mother's expression softened. "I want to keep you close, of course. Every mother does. But my heart goes out to Leah, alone there in a strange land with only Daniel. Charley and Miriam's visit will do her heart good, but I know she would like to see you and Susanna. If his aunt and uncle weren't going down, I could never afford to send you. It may be Providence, a solution to more than one problem."

"God's plan for us?"

"I don't know. Perhaps. You don't have to decide today, but I'd like to write Leah as soon as possible. She'll be waiting for an answer."

"When will Daniel's aunt and uncle be leaving?"

"Right after Christmas. Just as Charley and Miriam will be returning."

"I'll pray on it," Rebecca agreed. "But I still think that Dorcas—"

"What about me?" came a familiar voice from the hallway.

Surprised, Rebecca looked up to see her cousin

standing at the open bedroom door, arms folded over her apron. "Dorcas. You're early."

"I know." Dorcas came into the room. She was wearing a rose-colored dress that had once belonged to Aunt Martha and black stockings with a hole at the ankle. Dorcas's black leather shoes were old and scuffed and badly needed polish. "My mother said I could walk over and see if you needed help with the meal. She and Dat took the buggy to fetch Grossmama from Anna's."

"We're about ready." Hannah rose from the bed, smiling at her. "I'll go on down and take the ham out of the oven. I was just warming it. You girls can sit here for a few minutes and catch up on your week."

Rebecca groaned inwardly. She didn't want to be left alone with Dorcas. She would rather shut herself in the attic where she could have a minute's peace to think this through. And if she did want company, Dorcas would be the last person she wanted to visit with today.

"*Ya,* Aunt Hannah. I'd like that," her cousin said in her shrill voice, a voice that sometimes had the same effect on Rebecca as fingernails on a blackboard.

But, no matter how she felt, Rebecca couldn't be unkind to anyone. She forced a smile. "It's nice having your family share our Sunday meal."

Dorcas twisted her chapped hands. Her bony hands and feet were large in proportion to her thin body, and as long as Rebecca could remember, Dorcas had chewed at her knuckles when she was anxious. She was obviously uneasy today, because the skin was red and sore on the middle of her right index finger.

"And Caleb," Rebecca added, when the silence stretched between them.

"*Ya,* Caleb is coming." Dorcas flopped on the bed beside her.

"Amelia, too," Rebecca added. "I hope your *dat* is feeling better."

Dorcas sighed. "I think he likes it, having the broken leg and everyone taking care of him. Caleb comes every day to help around the farm."

"He's a thoughtful person," Rebecca agreed. *Did they* have *to talk about Caleb?*

Dorcas nibbled at her raw knuckle. "I suppose."

Rebecca glanced at her cousin sitting beside her, surprised by her tone. "You don't sound very enthusiastic about him. Don't you like Caleb?" She couldn't help herself. She had to find out if they were really serious about each other. "Please don't do that." She caught hold of Dorcas's hand. "Look at your poor finger. It makes me hurt just looking at it."

Dorcas pulled her hand back and tucked it under her. "Mam says the same thing. She tells me it will turn black and fall off, but it never does. Most of the time, I don't even know I'm doing it."

Rebecca couldn't help but feel sorry for Dorcas. She looked so unhappy. "What's wrong?" she asked.

Dorcas raised her hand to her mouth, then tucked it under her again. "I know you will think I'm silly. Mam says I shouldn't be so choosy. She says that Caleb is a good catch." She sighed again. Dorcas's eyes were large and caramel brown and framed with long, light brown lashes. They were her most attractive feature, but they weren't lovely today. Dorcas looked as though maybe she'd been crying.

"I'm listening," Rebecca said, really meaning it.

"Caleb's the only boy—*man,*" she corrected herself.

"The only man who's ever come to dinner, who's ever treated me like…" Her face flushed. "Well, you know. I'm not pretty like you and your sisters. Boys have never asked me to ride home from singings with them, and they've never tried to outbid each other to buy my pie at school auctions."

"Don't say such things," Rebecca protested, pulling Dorcas into her arms and hugging her. "There's nothing wrong with the way you look." The truth was, Dorcas finally having her front tooth fixed made a big difference in her appearance, but Rebecca didn't want to say that. "A person's looks shouldn't matter. It's what they are inside that counts."

"Shouldn't, but they do, and you know it." Dorcas pulled away. "I'll be thirty next November, and if I don't find a beau before that, people will call me an old maid."

"But you…" Rebecca's pulse quickened. "You don't like Caleb?"

"He's all right, I suppose." Dorcas frowned. "*Ya,* I do like him. I'm getting used to his face. You know, the scars. It used to frighten me looking at it, but not so much now. What really bothers me is he's…well…dull."

"Dull? Caleb?" The man who would walk a roof beam in the dark to rescue a woman? A father who threw himself wholeheartedly into sock fights with his daughter? Could they be talking about the same person?

Dorcas sighed dramatically. "He's *so* serious. I know he's not much older than me, but he *seems* old. Last time he came to supper, he wanted to tell me about something he was making at the shop. Some wood thing. He went on and on about it, and I had to sit there and pretend to be interested, even though I was bored to tears."

"Oh," Rebecca replied softly. "I didn't know you felt

that way about him." She glanced at her cousin hopefully. "So the two of you aren't courting?"

"Not yet, but we'd be bundling if Mam had her way. She's really trying to push me into marrying him. As soon as possible."

"She said that?"

Dorcas shrugged. "It isn't what she says, it's the way she smiles at him, and how she wants everyone to know that the new preacher is calling on me." Dorcas rubbed at her irritated knuckle. "What do you think, Rebecca? Should we court? Should I look toward marrying him?"

Rebecca felt sick. The lump in her stomach had become a dull ache. She knew what her answer would be if Caleb asked *her* to be his wife. Feeling the way she did, could she be honest with Dorcas? "Have you prayed about it? What does your heart tell you?"

"I don't know if it's my heart or my head," her cousin answered. "I'm scared. I'm afraid that if I say no, I'll end up living the rest of my life with my mother, with people feeling sorry for me. I'll be another Aunt Jezzy."

"But Aunt Jezzy found someone who treasures her," Rebecca reminded. "She's happy."

"But it didn't happen until she was old. I don't want to spend my life fetching and carrying for my mother. I love my parents, but I want my own home, and babies, lots of babies. Caleb could give me all that. I'd have to be stupid to refuse him."

"Is that a reason to marry a man?" Rebecca managed.

"Maybe," Dorcas said. "*Ya,* I think it is. I can respect Caleb and be thankful for what he can give me. If I keep his house and raise his daughter, friendship will grow between us." A smile spread across her face and she looked at Rebecca. "Thank you, Rebecca." She let out her breath. "I feel so relieved. I knew you'd give me good advice."

"But I haven't," Rebecca protested.

"In time, love will come." Dorcas got up off the bed. "That's what my mother says. Marriage first, work as a team and everything else will fall into place."

But not for me, Rebecca thought. *Not for me.*

Dinner with Caleb, Amelia, Dorcas and her family was as miserable for Rebecca as she feared it would be. Dorcas and Caleb were seated across from one another, and each seemed to take great pains to avoid looking at the other. Amelia whined and fussed her way through the meal, breaking into tears when she spilled her milk and when she put her sleeve in the mashed potatoes while reaching for a biscuit. Grossmama commented loudly on poorly behaved children and questioned Caleb at length on the size of his property and the extent of his mortgage.

"Would you be able to support my granddaughter?" she asked before he could answer. "She has no dowry, you know. But she's a fine seamstress, none better, certainly not her mother. Martha was never handy with a needle."

"Lovina," Mam soothed. "Let the man eat. You can question Caleb to your heart's content after he's finished his dessert."

Grossmama frowned, popped another forkful of ham into her mouth and chewed noisily. An awkward silence settled over the table, a lapse that Caleb attempted to fill by describing his unease when the police had stopped him and the boys in the Beachy buggy.

Irwin clapped a hand over his mouth and stifled a chuckle.

Dorcas didn't seem to hear. Doggedly, she kept eating her macaroni salad and pickled beets. And when Rebecca managed to catch her gaze, Dorcas pursed her lips and shrugged, as if to say, "Didn't I tell you he was boring?"

After everyone was done eating, Mam and Rebecca got up to clear away the dirty dishes so the pies and cakes could be served. The bishop and Uncle Reuben stepped out on the back porch to get some air and talk.

"I want cookies," Amelia demanded, although she'd barely touched anything on her plate.

"No dessert until you eat all of your dinner," Dorcas admonished.

Amelia screwed up her face and began to wail.

"It's not a problem," Rebecca said, reaching for Amelia's plate.

"You're spoiling her," Aunt Martha told Caleb. "What she needs is—"

Amelia twisted on the bench, caught her plate with her sleeve and knocked it onto the floor. The dish broke and mashed potatoes, ham and applesauce went flying. Amelia threw herself into the mess and began to sob.

Caleb reached for his daughter, amid angry whispers from Aunt Martha. Dorcas got to her first and scooped her up. "Hush, now, Amelia," she said. "No need to fuss so about a broken plate."

Amelia kicked and screamed. "Don't want you! Want Becca!"

Caleb's face flamed as he took her from Dorcas. "Quiet down," he said. But Amelia's tantrum continued. "I'm sorry," he said to Dorcas. "I'll take her home."

Susanna stared wide-eyed.

"Better take her out behind the barn and warm her bottom," Aunt Martha advised.

"Ne, ne," Hannah soothed. "She's tired and feeling out of sorts."

"Becca!" Amelia howled, struggling against her father's embrace. "I want…want…my Maaam."

"Shh, shh," Rebecca said, putting out her arms. "Give her to me, Caleb."

With a look of helplessness, he passed the crying child to her, and Amelia clung to Rebecca with all her strength.

"What's wrong?" Rebecca asked. "Are you tired?"

Amelia buried her head in Rebecca's neck and sobbed great wrenching sobs of anguish that lapsed into hiccups. Her little face felt hot and sweaty against Rebecca's skin.

"Shh, shh," Rebecca continued to murmur as she patted the child's back. "No wonder she's acting out," she said, meeting Caleb's worried gaze. "She's burning up. I think she's running a fever."

Chapter Fifteen

Hannah's forehead creased in a concerned expression as she placed a hand on Amelia's forehead. "She does feel as though she has a fever. 102, maybe 103. Poor baby," she crooned, kissing her forehead. "No wonder you're cross."

"Are you sure? Do you have a thermometer?" Caleb's irritation with his daughter's awful behavior vanished, instantly replaced with dread. "Should we take her to the emergency room?"

Hannah shook her head. "I don't think that will be necessary. Children get fevers. I don't believe her fever is high enough that you can't wait to decide tomorrow if you should call her doctor."

"She doesn't have one," Caleb said. "I've been meaning to find one for her, but I've been so busy since we got to Delaware and I kept putting it off."

Rebecca hugged Amelia to her. "We do have a thermometer."

Caleb glanced in her direction, remembering that she'd urged him more than once to choose a pediatrician for Amelia. To her credit, she didn't mention that now.

"Susanna," Rebecca called. "Can you get the thermometer from the downstairs bathroom cabinet?" She gave him a reassuring nod. "You can trust Mam. She's tended enough sick children to know."

Caleb shook his head. "I wouldn't have brought her here if I'd known she was ill. I can't remember the last time she ran a fever." Illness was one of the things that made him feel helpless with Amelia. "Give her to me," he said.

This time, Amelia went willingly and put her arms around his neck. "I want to go home," she whimpered. "I want my baby doll."

Susanna returned with the thermometer and a bottle of rubbing alcohol. Rebecca took both to the sink, poured a little alcohol over the thermometer to clean it before rinsing it with cool water. "Here, sweetie," she said to Amelia. "Put this under your tongue."

Caleb rocked his child against his chest. He loved this child with every fiber of his being. Just the thought that she might have something seriously wrong with her terrified him. "Just for a moment," he soothed. "Be a good girl and let Rebecca take your temperature."

Rebecca removed the thermometer and held it up to the light. "102 degrees," she pronounced. "Not good, but not dangerous, either. She could be coming down with an ear infection or a cold."

"Or the flu," Martha said helpfully.

"Lots of flu going around," Rebecca's *grossmama* agreed. "My Jonas had it bad in the fall."

Caleb didn't respond. Rebecca had explained that her grandmother Lovina's memory was spotty at best, and that she often believed that her son, Jonas, Hannah's late husband, was still alive. Furthermore, Rebecca explained, no one corrected the elderly woman because when Lovina did remember, she mourned Jonas's death as deeply as if he'd just passed on, rather than dying years ago.

"I don't believe Amelia has the flu," Hannah said. "She's not throwing up, and she's not complaining of aching joints. Rebecca could be right. It could be no more than a cold."

Caleb let out the breath he'd been unconsciously holding. A cold or an ear infection, he could deal with. "I'd best get her home," he said. "Into her bed." He looked back at Hannah. "Thank you for dinner."

"No such thing," Lovina stated firmly. "It's cold outside. Take that baby outside and she could die of an ague. Why take the chance when Jonas and Hannah have all these empty bedrooms? You can just tuck her into bed here."

"She's right, Caleb," Hannah agreed. "We can put Amelia into one of the spare rooms and we can help you care for her."

Caleb felt uncertain. He didn't want to be a bother, but neither did he want to risk taking his daughter out of a warm house into the frigid air. What if Lovina was right and exposure made her worse? "If you're sure I won't be putting you out."

"If she's got a fever in the afternoon, you can be certain it will go higher tonight." Martha bustled around the table and gave Dorcas a small shove in his direction. "You and Amelia should stay here, Caleb. That way, Dorcas can assist you. It wouldn't be proper, her going to your house. My Reuben's always been careful of Dorcas's reputation, especially now that you've done her the honor of paying court to her."

Caleb didn't know what to say. "I'm not— We're not—" he began, but Dorcas cut him off.

"Ya," she agreed, giving him the most genuine smile he'd ever seen on her face. "It's *gut,* you and me talking like we are. It makes me pleased. But it wouldn't be right, me taking care of your Amelia." Her eyes glistened with hope. "Since we aren't strictly a couple yet."

Caleb didn't know what to say to clear things up without embarrassing her further, but he didn't want to give anyone the wrong impression, either. So he just repeated what Dorcas had said. "You're right, we aren't a couple yet." And then he added, "Nothing decided between us."

Dorcas lowered her head and blushed. "That's what I've been trying to get Mam to understand. We haven't come to an understanding yet. We're not really courting, just considering the possibility."

"Nonsense," Lovina insisted. "Of course you're courting. Dorcas is perfect for you. She's a preacher's daughter, isn't she? And she's been brought up properly." She glanced pointedly at Rebecca. "Not like Hannah's girls. A preacher has to remember his position. Dorcas is for you, Caleb Wittner, and the sooner you two quit stalling and cry the banns, the better."

Caleb didn't know what to say. No one seemed to notice.

"You don't think Amelia will be sick to her stomach, do you?" Dorcas's eyes widened as she backed away from him and Amelia. "I'm not much for tending sick people. If she throws up…" She shuddered. "I'd probably throw up, too." She covered her face with her hands. "I'm sorry, I just can't."

"No matter," Hannah said. "We'll manage just fine."

She motioned to Caleb. "Bring the child into the bedroom and we'll get her tucked in."

"I have Fritzy at home, and my livestock." He looked down at Amelia. How small she seemed. Wisps of damp hair clung to her bright red cheeks. "I'm not sure what to do. I can't just leave."

"Irwin can go and get Fritzy, and Amelia's baby doll," Rebecca suggested. "I know right where it is. And he can do your evening chores, can't you, Irwin?"

"Ya." Irwin, still at the table, looked up from forking another piece of sweet-potato pie into his mouth.

"It's the least he can do." Hannah led the way past the parlor to one of her downstairs bedrooms. "If it wasn't for you, Caleb, Irwin would be in a lot more trouble than he is now."

Caleb followed Hannah's directions and tucked Amelia into a bed in a spacious room across from the downstairs bath. He'd never seen the private areas of Hannah's home before, but he was comforted by the homey feel of the chamber. The walls here were a pale blue, the furniture old and lovingly polished until the worn grain shone softly in the lamplight. A yellow-and-blue braid rug and several hand-worked quilts added color.

"Used to be my room," Lovina informed him as she walked into the bedroom behind them, her cane tapping. She settled herself into a high-backed rocking chair. "Before I went to live with Anna."

Hannah looked questioningly at her mother-in-law.

"You just have that Irwin boy go by Anna's and tell her I'm staying here with this sick child. Can't have the new preacher here alone with you and my granddaughters."

"Lovina—" Hannah began.

Rebecca's *grossmama* cut her off with a wave of her cane. "Oh, I know you think my mind wanders. Sometimes it does, but I'm staying as long as Caleb does, and that's that." She turned her cane around and used the hand grip to drag a footstool closer. "I'll prop my feet up and be as comfy as a hen in a nest."

Hannah stood in the doorway and sighed. "Of course, you're welcome to stay if you wish, Mam."

The older woman scowled. "Lovina. I'm not your mother."

Hannah averted her eyes. "*Ya*, Lovina." Going to a blanket chest, she removed a blanket and spread it over Lovina. "If there's anything you want—"

"If there's anything I need, he can fetch it for me. He'll have little enough to do, sitting here and watching the child sleep."

Hannah backed out of the room as Caleb drew an oak desk chair up beside the bed. Amelia's face looked pale against the pillow, but she was already getting sleepy. "Are you warm enough?" he asked.

"Don't leave me, Dat."

He pulled a soft blue coverlet up to her chin. "I won't, pumpkin." Caleb continued to stroke Amelia's hair. There was no sound but the child's breathing and the patter of sleet against the window.

"It's a fine thing you're doing, courting our Dorcas," Lovina said in her thin, raspy voice. "She never was as pretty as Hannah's girls, but pretty don't last. Dorcas will make you a *gut* wife."

Caleb didn't answer.

"We'd given her up for an old maid," Lovina continued. "Many a time she'd come crying to me, saying no decent man would ever have her. But I told her that God would see to her. I told her to pray for a husband, and here you come, a man with a solid house, two good hands and a voice for praising the Lord. He sent you to Dorcas, and don't you forget it."

"I haven't made up my mind yet," he said cautiously. "Dorcas is a fine young woman, but I'm not certain."

"None of that talk," Lovina warned, shaking an arthritic finger at him. "You drop her like a hot potato and it will break her heart. No decent man comes to her mother's table three weeks in a row and doesn't pop the question."

The creak of door hinges caught Caleb's attention and he glanced toward the hallway. Rebecca stood there, a basin of water in her hands. "I thought that a cool washcloth on her forehead might help."

"Go on with you, Rebecca," Lovina chastised. "The preacher and I are having a private talk about his marriage to Dorcas. You go find Jonas and help him with the milking. You're not needed here."

Rebecca set the basin and a clean washcloth and towel on the nightstand beside the bed.

Caleb looked up at her. "Stay," he said.

"No place for you." Lovina puckered up her mouth. "Dorcas should be here, being Caleb's intended," she muttered, seemingly speaking more to herself than to him or Rebecca now. "My Martha's right. Her *kapp*'s set for Preacher Wittner."

Before Caleb could think of how to stop her, Rebecca quietly slipped from the room, leaving him alone with Amelia and Lovina. The elderly woman soon dozed off. And then he had nothing to do but sit, worry about his sick child and try to think about how to untie the tangled reins of his life.

Blinking back tears, Rebecca returned to the kitchen. No one was there but Dorcas, who was putting on her cloak by the back door. "Are you leaving?" she asked.

"Oh, Rebecca!"

To her surprise, Dorcas threw herself into her arms. *"Danke. Danke,"* Dorcas said, hugging her fiercely. "I know it should be me with his girl, but I just can't!"

"It's nothing," Rebecca answered, hugging her back. "You know sick children don't bother me. And I adore Amelia."

Dorcas didn't let go. "Not just for this, for Caleb. For helping me see what's best, for helping me accept God's plan for me," she whispered.

Rebecca pried her cousin's hands loose and stepped back. She forced a weak smile.

"I'd have to be stupid to refuse him, wouldn't I? This is my chance. I have to take it, or I'll spend the rest of my life regretting it." Dorcas tugged her faded cloak into place and began to tie the string at the throat. "I'll get used to his face. I know I will. And he's a kind man, a man of substance that I can respect. It will be a good marriage."

Rebecca's heart sank. *Ne. Not you,* she wanted to say. *I want him for my husband!* But she couldn't. She couldn't bear to see the happiness on Dorcas's face turn to anguish. "If Caleb asks you," she reminded softly. "Nothing is decided yet. Not really."

"Not yet," Dorcas said. "But soon. Mam will insist on it. The season for weddings is past, but Caleb is a widower. We can marry whenever we please, the sooner the better, really. What do I need with a big wedding?"

"Dorcas!" Hannah called from the porch. "Your parents are waiting in the buggy."

"I have to go," Dorcas said. "I'll come again tomorrow to see how Amelia is. I'm sure it's nothing, just a cold. But I'll pray for her."

Rebecca nodded. "*Ya.* Prayer helps."

Her mother came into the kitchen and wiped her shoes on the mat. "Still nasty out there," Hannah told Dorcas as she went out the door. "Tell your father to be careful on the road. Blacktop may be slippery." She closed the door behind Dorcas and turned. "I definitely think you should go to Leah," she said firmly. "Give Caleb time to make his choice."

"I think you're right," Rebecca said. She looked down at the floor, then back up at her mother. "I'll go, but please, don't tell anyone. Let me decide when."

Hannah's shoulders slumped. "Daughter, daughter. How does that make it any easier on either of you?"

"Not yet, Mam, please. Amelia is what's important now. I promise I won't do anything rash. Just let me have a little more time to make certain that Amelia's Christmas isn't ruined. I won't be alone with Caleb, and I won't give anyone reason to think ill of either of us." She went to the cupboard and took down a white pottery pitcher. "Caleb will need cool water, in case Amelia is thirsty."

Hannah nodded. "All right. Just as long as you remember that happiness can't ever be found in the ashes of someone else's unhappiness."

A single tear welled up and splashed down Rebecca's

cheek, but she turned away so that her mother wouldn't see it. "I keep telling myself that," she murmured. "Over and over."

Sometime after 2:00 a.m., Amelia's fever did rise higher, and together, while Grossmama slept on in her chair, Rebecca and Caleb cared for the sick child. They took turns holding her and wiping her forehead and body with cool washcloths, fed her sips of willow bark tea and baby aspirin.

"This is all my fault," Caleb confided when Amelia fell asleep in his arms. "I should never have brought her to dinner. I should have noticed that she wasn't feeling well when she didn't eat her breakfast."

Rebecca sat on the edge of the bed. The weather outside had changed from sleet to rain, and now a downpour rattled against the windows as the wind whipped around the house. She was tired and concerned for Amelia, but she cherished this time together, just the two of them. Not that they were alone. Her grandmother was here, preserving moral decency, and Hannah came in from time to time to check on the patient.

Rebecca kept her promise to her mother foremost in her mind. She and Caleb talked only about Amelia or everyday things that any neighbor might share. Twice, Caleb had read passages from the Bible, and they had prayed together for Amelia's safe recovery. They had been careful that they didn't sit too close or touch each other, yet she had never been more conscious of him as a man.

She rejoiced in the tenderness that Caleb showed toward Amelia. The only light in the room came from two propane lanterns, and the radiance of the love shining in Caleb's eyes as he looked down at his daughter. If Dorcas could see him now, Rebecca thought, she wouldn't see the scars that twisted the surface of his face, she would only see the goodness of this man and the depth of his character.

Selfishly, Rebecca was glad that Dorcas wasn't here. This was her time, and no matter what happened in the future, whether they could ever be together or not, no one could take this memory from her.

By 3:00 a.m., the fever had broken and the crisis had passed. An hour later, when Rebecca fetched warm water to bathe the sweat from Amelia's throat and chest, a small sprinkling of a rash was evident on the child's skin. "Look at that," Rebecca said.

"What is it?" Caleb asked.

"I'm not sure. It doesn't look like chicken pox or measles. We can take her to a doctor in the morning, but maybe it doesn't matter exactly what it is. Children get all kinds of things. What does matter is that her fever is gone and her color is better."

"You're sure?" Caleb demanded. "You're sure she's—"

"Dat." Amelia's eyelashes fluttered, and then opened wide. A smile spread across her face. "Dat, I'm hungry."

"You're hungry?" he asked in disbelief. "What do you want to eat?"

"Hush up," Grossmama wheezed. "I'm trying to sleep. She told you the fever had passed, didn't she? Men." She groaned, drifted off and began to snore again.

Rebecca met Caleb's gaze and stifled a giggle. "You heard her, didn't you?" she whispered. She smiled down at Amelia. "How about if I make you some toast with strawberry jam?"

"Ya," Amelia said. "And hot chocolate."

Rebecca shook her head. "No chocolate yet. Maybe some tea with honey."

"Okay."

Caleb reached over and clasped her hand. "Thank you," he said. "Without you…" His voice choked with emotion. "Rebecca." He swallowed visibly. "Rebecca, what are we going to do?"

She lifted her lashes to look at him in the dim light. Grossmama and Amelia were both present, but it suddenly seemed as if it was only she and Caleb. *"Do?* About what?"

He looked down at Amelia. "Rebecca and I will get your toast and jam. We'll be right back, sweetie." He rose from his chair, took Rebecca's hand and led her out of the room. He closed the door before he spoke again, keeping his voice low. No one else seemed to be awake in the house, but it was obvious he wanted their conversation to remain private.

"About us," he said. "What are we going to do about us?"

"Us?" she repeated. Her voice sounded breathy. Did he mean what she thought he meant?

He groaned aloud. "Must I say it?" he whispered. "What are we to do about these feelings between us? I've tried to deny them and I think you have, as well, but after tonight, I feel…"

Rebecca looked away from him. Part of her heart was singing; she had not been mistaken. Caleb *did* care for her. But part of her heart was breaking. What did he mean what were they going to *do?* They were going to do nothing. He was going to do the right thing. How could Caleb *not* propose to Dorcas? He had let the matter go on too long. Rebecca felt as if *she* had let it go too far. She could never hurt Dorcas or shame her family by stealing Caleb out from under her cousin.

Rebecca returned her gaze to Caleb's face. "What will we do?" she asked, slowly taking her hand from his. "What we have been doing. What is right. Trying to live as the faith teaches us."

This time, Caleb was the one who looked away. "Are you telling me you don't feel the same—"

She reached out and squeezed his big, warm shoulder, silencing him. Then she released him. She was afraid that if she didn't let go of him now, she would never be able to let go of him. "Dorcas expects you to ask to marry her. Her mother and father, Grossmama… Everyone, Caleb, expects you to ask Dorcas to marry you." She pressed her lips together, afraid she might cry, willing herself not to. "I can't hurt my cousin. And neither can you."

He hung his head. "You're right," he whispered. "I'm sorry."

"There's nothing to be sorry for. We've done nothing wrong, Caleb. Nothing to be ashamed of." Her voice quavered. "But this has to stop. Now." She took a deep breath. "You need to find someone else to look after your house." Her voice cracked. "And Amelia."

"But Amelia loves you."

"It's not fair to her. She should begin getting to know Dorcas. You'll have to find someone else to work for you until you can be wed." She almost blurted out that she was going to Brazil but she couldn't bring herself to do it. Instead, Rebecca made herself walk down the hall, away from Caleb. "I'll stay until Christmas, then I'm done."

Chapter Sixteen

It was just after lunch on December 24, the day before Christmas, and Rebecca was scrubbing the kitchen countertops in Caleb's house. She and Amelia had made trays of Moravian sand tarts, cinnamon crisps and black walnut cookies. Together, they'd packed assortments into brown paper bags, tied them with green yarn bows and were preparing to deliver them as gifts to her mother, sisters and their families.

Naturally, there would be holiday excitement and visiting at each home, so the process might take all afternoon. Rebecca was determined to leave the house and kitchen spotless, especially because she knew this would be her last day here. Wiping her hands on her apron, she paused to look around. Everything was in its place: dishes dried and put away, a chicken potpie staying warm on the back of the stove and the floor shiny clean.

She glanced at the large, colorful wall calendar with its cheerful painting of an old-fashioned, horse-drawn sled crossing a snowy farm field and felt a twinge of guilt. Where had the month of December gone? Every morning when she came to Caleb's, she'd meant to tell him that she would be leaving for Brazil a few days after Christmas. But somehow, it had never seemed the right moment. Rebecca's promise to her mother weighed heavily on her conscience, but still she'd held her secret, wanting just a few more days. The fault was hers and she took full responsibility, but Caleb hadn't made her unpleasant task any easier.

Amelia's illness that had worried them so had passed as quickly as most children's ailments. Her pediatrician diagnosed the rash as roseola. Children her age were generally too old to contract it, but the doctor had told Caleb there was nothing to worry about. Within a week the rash was gone and Amelia had been as bubbly as ever.

Caleb was a different story.

Since the night of Amelia's illness and the confession that Rebecca and Caleb had shared in the hallway, he had barely spoken to Rebecca. Before Amelia's fever, Caleb had often shown a lighthearted side. They'd laughed together over small things, and he'd brought home from the shop fine articles of woodwork to show her. He'd even told her about the doll cradle for Amelia's beloved doll and the small four-wheeled cart that Fritzy could pull that he was making for her for Christmas. Not only had Rebecca not seen Amelia's Christmas gifts, but when she'd hinted that she wanted to stop by to see the progress, Caleb had told her to stay away from the chair shop. He'd even started packing his lunch the night before and carrying it with him, putting an end to her and Amelia walking over at noon to bring him a hot meal. Now the only time he attempted a conversation with Rebecca was when he was forced to discuss a household matter, or one that related to Amelia.

"I'm ready! Can we go now? Can we?" Amelia dashed into the room with Fritzy right behind her.

"Ya," Rebecca answered. Her heart warmed at the sight of the child. It seemed as if she was growing every day, no longer a baby but a strong and healthy girl. How different Amelia seemed from what she'd been when Rebecca had first come to work for Caleb. The sulking and sullen face had been replaced by smiles and an eagerness to learn new skills and make new friends. Parting with Amelia would be so painful…as painful as parting with Caleb.

Rebecca knelt to retie Amelia's shoe and apron. How neat she looked in her new blue dress, white apron and black stockings. Mam had fashioned a white *kapp* just Amelia's size, and Susanna had carefully starched and ironed it. The hooded cloak was Rebecca's Christmas gift. It was calf-length, navy blue wool, lined against the cold and hand sewn with tiny, almost invisible stitches.

Amelia hugged her. "I love you, Becca," she cried.

Rebecca pulled the child into her arms and swallowed hard. "I love you, too, Amelia," she murmured. If only things were different, she thought, this would be her very own daughter.

Not that she'd completely given up hope. Because she truly believed God had a plan for her. But neither she nor Caleb had spoken of what had happened that night. Sometimes, she wondered if she'd imagined the whole thing. Caleb continued to accept Aunt Martha's invitation to Wednesday-night suppers. With every passing day, it had become clearer to Rebecca that Mam was right—she couldn't keep working for Caleb, feeling the way she did about him. She and Susanna would go to visit Leah, and when they came home, maybe…

The back door opened and the big poodle ran barking to welcome Caleb home. Rebecca looked up from where she was still kneeling on the floor. "Caleb? Is that you?"

"Who else would it be?" He removed his hat and hung it on a hook by the door. He looked at Amelia. "What are you doing down there?"

"Dat! Dat! We made cookies!" Amelia bounced from one foot to another. "We're taking them to Anna's and—"

"It's bitter cold. I'm not sure you should go out in this wind," Caleb said.

Hastily, Rebecca got to her feet. "We were going to deliver our Christmas cookies. I have our buggy, and I promise to keep her bundled up."

Caleb pushed a big cloth bag with something heavy in it into Rebecca's hands. "For you," he said brusquely.

"Thank you." She'd made him a fruitcake, but it was at home. Mam had invited Caleb and Amelia to come by tomorrow for dinner.

There was no Christmas Day church service. There would be family prayers and Bible readings in the morning, but the afternoon would be shared with friends and family. They would exchange gifts, sing songs together and enjoy each other's company. Most of the gifts were practical ones, but Mam always managed to provide something special for each of them. On Christmas, it was the men who washed dishes and made coffee, and the women sat around the stove and teased them.

"Are you going to look and see what it is?" Caleb stroked his close-cut beard.

Heart pounding, Rebecca reached into the bag and

retrieved a cedar box inlaid with hearts and tulips in darker pieces of cherry, oak and walnut. The box was about twelve by fourteen inches and fastened with brass hinges and a brass latch. "Oh, Caleb, it's beautiful," she exclaimed. The box smelled of cedar, and she could see the hours of patient craftsmanship that had gone into making it. "It's wonderful."

"Nothing much," he said. "For your Bible." He absently rubbed the scarred side of his face as he scanned the stove. "There's no dinner?"

Rebecca clasped the box against her. "I...I didn't expect you. Didn't you take your lunch this morning?"

"I did, but I didn't have time for breakfast. I ate my sandwich." He scowled. "You and Amelia must have eaten something. Isn't there anything left?" His mouth formed a tight line.

Anger made her answer sharply. "Do you think I'm one of those snake-charming, crystal-ball-gazing gypsy women with rings in their ears? How was I supposed to know you'd come home and want lunch?"

He started to speak, but she didn't let him.

"Amelia and I had peanut-butter sandwiches and apple slices. You're welcome to that if you want to make your own. I promised her that we'd deliver our Christmas cookies, and that's what we're going to do."

He looked stricken. "*Ya*...but..."

"But nothing, Caleb. Thank you for the Bible box. It's the nicest thing anyone has ever given me." She glanced down at Amelia. "Honey, I think you need your gloves. Be a good girl and go upstairs and fetch them." Once Amelia had scampered off, Rebecca took a breath and then blurted out what she'd been holding back for weeks. "I'm going to Brazil. To spend three months with my sister. I'm leaving the day after tomorrow."

"Brazil?" He couldn't have looked any more shocked if she'd told him that she was going to the moon. "You can't go to Brazil. I haven't found anyone to take care of Amelia yet."

"I told you weeks ago that I would only be working for you until Christmas. You've had plenty of time to find a replacement for me, Caleb." Her lower lip trembled, but her voice did not. "I have an opportunity to go to Brazil, and I'm going. And I think it's better this way—since you can't make up your mind whether you're courting my cousin or not."

"You're just leaving us? Abandoning Amelia when she's come to trust you? Abandoning *us?*" Caleb's voice choked with emotion and his eyes clouded with tears. Was he losing the woman he loved? Again? His first instinct was to forbid her to leave. "Rebecca. You can't go. I won't let you."

"Ne, Caleb," she answered. "It isn't up to you. I've made up my mind."

"This isn't fair."

"Ne, it isn't. Not to me. Not to Amelia, and certainly not to Dorcas. I'm going to my sister's, and while I'm gone, you can work out your own problems."

"But it's Christmas. I made the box for you. I thought…"

"I don't know what you thought." Rebecca folded her arms and glared at him. "How could I know *what* you think? You never say anything to me anymore."

"You must know…" Why were the words so hard for him? Why did it feel as though his world was crumbling? "…how much I care for you. I told you that night."

"And I told you that I care for you, but I can't hurt Dorcas and—"

Fritzy began to bark and scratch against the back door. Caleb heard the sound of a horse's hoofbeats and the creak of buggy wheels in the yard and went to the window in the utility room. "Someone's here," he said to Rebecca. "We'll talk about this later."

"*Ne,* we won't. I've said my piece," she replied. "If there's more you want to say, tell me when I get back from Brazil." She reached for her coat on the hook. "There's a chicken potpie for your supper. I'll bring Amelia home after we deliver the cookies."

He was still looking out the window. "It's Martha and Dorcas." *Not them,* he thought. He couldn't face them now—not when he was losing Rebecca. If only he'd told them weeks ago that Dorcas and he would never make a good match. He'd wanted to. He would have if it hadn't been for the happy expression on Dorcas's face that first Wednesday he'd come to supper. He'd seen something of himself there, had known what it felt like to be unwanted.

His childhood had been lonely, and he'd often wondered if he'd ever make a place for himself where he felt at home. When he looked at Dorcas, he saw the lanky, awkward boy he'd been, with big feet and bony shoulders, the man-child who'd been taken in out of duty rather than love.

Dorcas was a decent girl, getting no younger, ruled by an overbearing mother and shunned by eligible suitors in the community. Caleb had sensed that she had a loving heart, even if she sometimes spoke out thoughtlessly. She wasn't as pretty or as clever as Rebecca, but she was a devout daughter of the church. She had as much right as any other young woman to be a wife. And now, because he hadn't had the courage to reject her, things had escalated and people believed that his intentions were serious.

How could he have been such a fool? All the time he was searching for someone to fill the emptiness in his life, Rebecca had been right there in front of him. He'd misjudged her badly. He hadn't thought that she was the proper choice for a preacher, the one to heal his grief and fill his life with joy.

"Rebecca, wait," he said. "We can still fix this."

She stopped and met his gaze. "At what cost, Caleb? Do you think we could ever be happy if we break Dorcas's heart?" She glanced back toward the interior of the house. "Amelia! Let's go, sweetie!"

"Rebecca, please," Caleb said. He reached out to take her arm but she brushed past him, opened the back door and stepped from the utility room out onto the open back porch.

"Just the person I wanted to see," Martha said, trudging toward them. "*Ne,* not you, Caleb. My niece. We need to talk. Privately."

As she approached, Caleb saw that Martha's eyes were swollen and bloodshot. She looked as if she'd been crying. "What's wrong?" he asked. "Has something happened to Reuben?"

Martha's chin quivered and she brought a man's handkerchief to her nose and blew loudly. "I just need to…talk to Rebecca."

Bewildered, Caleb looked from her to a grim-faced

Dorcas standing beside the buggy. "You're welcome to come into the house, too," he said to her.

"I want to talk to you," Dorcas called to him. "Alone."

"What is it? Is someone ill?" Wind cut through Caleb's shirt. He'd come out without his coat and the temperature was freezing. It was beginning to snow. Big flakes were falling on the ground, the horse and the buggy.

Dorcas shook her head. "The problem is you."

"Me?" He looked from Dorcas to Martha to Rebecca, then back at Dorcas. "Maybe we'd all better go inside," he suggested.

"Get in the buggy." Dorcas climbed back in.

"All right." He glanced toward the house, wondering if he should go back for his coat, but Martha was already pushing past him on the porch and through the doorway into the utility room. Deciding that freezing to death might be the lesser of evils, he hurried to the closed buggy and got up into the seat beside Dorcas. "What's wrong?" he asked her.

"Everything." She looked at him and scowled. "Where's your coat? Do you want to take pneumonia?"

He rubbed his hands together. "Say what you've come to say."

"Very well." She looked him in the eye. "I've come to break off our courtship."

Caleb blinked, certain he had misunderstood. "What?"

"You heard me." She held up her hand. "And you can't change my mind." Her cloth gloves were worn, one finger mended with an off-color thread. Her nose glowed scarlet in the cold.

"Dorcas."

"Now hear me out, Caleb. I don't mean to hurt you. You're a good, respectable man, even a passable preacher, although your sermons are still too short. But the truth is, I'm not romantically attracted to you, and I never will be."

He stared. Had she just said what he thought he'd heard? "I don't—"

Dorcas's right palm rose inches from his face, cutting him off in midsentence. "Give me the courtesy to allow me to finish. You won't change my mind." She pressed her chapped lips together. "I know that this will disappoint you. And I know that you may be my last chance to find a husband—not to mention how upset my parents are. But I refuse to settle."

"I—"

She eyed him sternly and then went on. "Think me foolish if you like, but I want a marriage like Ruth has, like Anna, Johanna and Miriam. I want what my Yoder cousins have. And if God doesn't send me a man that I can love with my whole heart, then it's clear He intends for me to remain single."

In the kitchen, Rebecca pulled out a chair and helped her weeping Aunt Martha into it. "What is it?" Rebecca asked. She'd never seen Aunt Martha cry. "Has something bad happened? Please tell me. You're scaring me."

Aunt Martha buried her face in her hands. She was still wearing her heavy wool cloak and bonnet. She'd refused to take them off.

Amelia and Fritzy wandered into the kitchen. Amelia was eating a cinnamon crisp. "Are we going now?" she asked.

"Not yet." Rebecca waved the child away. "I'm talking to Aunt Martha. Go up to your room and play. I'll call you when we're ready." She didn't let her argue. "Please do as I say, Amelia."

With a grimace, Amelia retraced her steps. Fritzy followed her, eyes watching the floor in case a crumb dropped.

"Now." Rebecca returned to stand beside her aunt and placed a hand on her shoulder. "Tell me what's wrong."

Aunt Martha groaned. "It's my Dorcas."

"She's not sick, is she?"

Aunt Martha shifted her black-rimmed glasses lower, turned her head and peered up over the top of them. "Dorcas is breaking off with Caleb."

"What?" Weak-kneed, Rebecca dropped into the chair nearest her aunt.

"I know it's hard to believe, but Dorcas refuses to court him. She's breaking the news to him now. Her father is furious."

"Uncle Reuben is furious?" Rebecca hadn't heard Uncle Reuben take a stand on anything as long as she could remember. She concentrated on what her aunt had just said, and hope made her heart race. "Dorcas doesn't want to marry Caleb?" she repeated woodenly.

"Are you deaf? It's what I said, isn't it?"

Rebecca nodded.

"I want her to be happy. My only daughter. Why wouldn't I?" Aunt Martha tugged on the strings of her black hat. "Foolish of me, I know." Her lower lip quivered. "What will we do if Caleb causes a scandal? He'll be disappointed, I know."

"Uncle Reuben?"

"Not your uncle," Aunt Martha replied sharply.

"*Caleb*. Caleb will be disappointed. How will it look for his position? People will say she dumped him." She lowered her voice to a whisper. "That there's something wrong with him. More than the obvious," she added.

"Maybe not," Rebecca ventured.

"Oh, they will. I can hear it now. Everyone will be trying to guess what secret he's hiding." Martha rocked back and forth, a picture of misery. "A disaster. But I have to stand by my daughter. If she won't listen to reason, then we must make the best of her decision."

Rebecca reached for her aunt's hand. "You mean you and Uncle Reuben won't try to force her to reconsider Caleb?"

"What kind of mother do you think I am? I'm not like my *mam*." Aunt Martha's eyes narrowed. "Dorcas thinks Caleb's dull. As boring as dried peas without pork fat, she said."

Rebecca started to defend Caleb and then thought better of it.

Her aunt glanced around and continued in a whisper. "You think I'm old and sour, but I had a young man once. Barnabas Troyer. We were young, and he was poor. Didn't even own a horse. Poorer even than we were, but we loved each other. Not a foolish fancy, but real love."

Compassion made her squeeze Aunt Martha's hand.

Martha sniffed and pried her hand loose. "Barnabas begged me to marry him, said we'd move to Missouri and start over, but I listened to my parents. I let him get away."

Rebecca exhaled softly. "I didn't know."

"Of course, you didn't. How would you know? How would anyone know? Eventually, I married Reuben. And you know how he is. A good enough man, a preacher, even, but never going to set the world on fire. Oh, we manage, all right. But, I'll say it once and never again. Your uncle was never one for hard work. It's his only weakness." She shook her head. "Mine was not taking real love when I found it."

Rebecca's heart was pounding so hard that she imagined Aunt Martha could hear it.

"I want more for Dorcas than making do. No matter what people say about her or our new preacher, I'm behind her one hundred percent. If she doesn't want to marry him, then she doesn't have to."

Rebecca's head was spinning. "But…why did you want to tell me?"

Aunt Martha lifted her head. "Because I know you can sway him. For whatever reason, he seems to listen to you. You need to make sure he doesn't make a fuss of this. Over my Dorcas rejecting him. Another woman will come along. He's a decent enough catch. Even with the—" she indicated the left side of her face "—you know."

"I—" Rebecca didn't know what to say. She could hardly believe what she was hearing.

"Maybe you should think about it. You're not getting any younger, you know." Aunt Martha rose. "Anyway, you'll have to forget all this nonsense about going to Brazil. You can't think of yourself, Rebecca. Your family needs you."

Five minutes later a stunned Rebecca and Caleb stood alone on the back porch as Aunt Martha's buggy rolled away through the falling snow. Speechless, Rebecca handed Caleb his coat that she'd snatched off the hook when she'd followed her aunt out of the house.

He slipped into it. "It's snowing," he said, turning back to her.

"Ya." She looked up into his eyes. "It is."

His cold hand closed around her waist and he pulled her into his arms. "I think I've been dumped," he murmured into her hair.

Trembling, she nodded. He smelled of cedar, wood chips, leather and molasses. She rested her head against his chest, not caring that allowing such liberties was reckless. She wanted to seize this moment and hold it forever. How right it felt, how safe and proper. How perfect.

"So I'm a free man," he continued.

"Ya, Caleb," she whispered. "I think you must be."

He tilted her chin up with cold fingers and pressed his warm lips against hers. The tender touch of his mouth and the nearness of him overwhelmed her and she felt giddy. "How will it look?" he asked.

"Look?" She blinked as clouds of snowflakes whirled around them.

A deep chuckle of laughter shook his chest. "Me, a preacher of the church, here alone with a beautiful woman on Christmas Eve? I suppose we'll have to remedy that and make it proper."

Hope made her daring, and she raised her head to meet his second kiss: tender, sweet and full of promise. "How could you make this proper?"

"Must I spell it out for you, girl?"

She smiled up at him through her tears of joy. "I think you must."

"Will you be my wife, Rebecca Yoder? Will you

marry me and make me the happiest man in Kent County?"

"Just Kent County?"

A grin spread across his face. "I was going to say the happiest man in Delaware, but I thought that you'd accuse me of pride. And pride is not a good trait for a man of God."

"You mention marriage, but not love." She pressed her lips together. "Do you love me, Caleb?"

"I love you, and I want you to be my wife and Amelia's mother—as soon as the banns can be called."

"What?" she teased, already thinking the same thing. "No courting?"

"Rebecca, darling, don't you know? We've been courting since the evening when I saved you in my barn."

She laid her palm gently over the scarred side of his face and gazed up into his dark eyes. "Or, maybe," she ventured, "maybe I saved you."

The intensity of his embrace nearly took her breath away. "Say you'll be my wife, Rebecca, or we're both in a great deal of trouble."

"*Ya,* Caleb," she replied. "I'll marry you, but it will have to wait until I get back from Brazil. I promised my sister. Three months, and then we'll be together."

"All right," he agreed. "You drive a hard bargain, but I've waited a long time. A little longer won't matter."

"Dat!" Amelia called, coming out onto the porch. "It's snowing! And we have to deliver our cookies for Christmas!"

"So we do," Caleb answered and then met Rebecca's gaze again. "Together, as a family."

And that's exactly what they did.

them with the right.

"... until next year." Caleb asked grandparents ...

this. "Warm enough?"

"Ya," Rebecca said softly. "Melt warm. And we wouldn't be warm, their parents and uncles ..."

Epilogue

Christmas Eve, one year later

"**A**re you warm enough?" Caleb looked both ways before guiding the horse and buggy onto the blacktop. He, Rebecca and Amelia were on their way home after making several Christmas Eve visits to elderly members of their church community. He'd wanted to make certain that no one was alone or in need tonight. They'd brought pies, vegetable soup and apples to give as token gifts, and perhaps most important, they'd taken time to visit at each stop.

"*Ya,* Dat." Amelia's small voice came from the back of the buggy where she was snuggled down under a quilt with Fritzy and a new addition to the family, Joy.

The half poodle, half lab puppy, a stray that Rebecca's sister Grace had rescued and nursed back to health, had been an early Christmas gift for his daughter. When Grace and Rebecca had hatched the plan, he'd been a little skeptical, because he didn't know how Fritzy would take to a new dog. He should have known better. Most of Rebecca's ideas were good ones, and it was a toss-up as to whether Amelia or Fritzy was more taken with the pup.

"What about you?" Caleb asked, glancing over at his wife. "Warm enough?"

"*Ya,* Caleb," she answered. "Toasty warm. And why wouldn't I be in my new mittens and scarf?"

He'd found the scarf on a trip to the mall with some of the boys he'd taken under his wing after the incident the winter before. The scarf was long and blue, and as soft as duck down. The color was a little brighter than some might think suitable for a preacher's wife, but the price and practicality of the gift made it impossible to pass up. And fancy scarf or not, no one could find fault with Rebecca as a role model for other young women.

"I was wrong," he admitted. "When I thought you were too flighty."

Rebecca didn't answer. That was something else he valued about her. As quick as she was to stand up for herself or give an opinion, she knew when to listen and let a man say what was on his mind.

"When Clarence Troyer had to have his appendix out, you offered to keep their five children so that Margaret could stay at the hospital with him through it all," Caleb said. "And when Susan King wanted to die at home, it was you who organized the neighborhood women so that someone was always with her and Paul, day and night."

"It was little enough to do for them."

Caleb slipped his arm around her shoulders and pulled her closer to him on the seat. Their legs pressed against one another under the lap robe, and his heart swelled with happiness that he'd found this woman to be his partner and the mother of his child. "I misjudged you, Rebecca. I thought that a devout woman had to be a serious one, but I was wrong about that, too." He leaned nearer and kissed her forehead. "You've made my house a home," he whispered hoarsely, "and I love you for it."

"The two of us, working together as a team." Rebecca smiled. "That's what makes the difference. You and me and Amelia, a real family."

"Am I a good husband?" he asked. "Do I make you happy?"

"Every day I thank God for bringing you to me."

He chuckled and flicked the reins over the horse's back. "I've wondered, but I was afraid to ask if you were disappointed in me."

"Never. You're strong and smart and—"

"A little stuffy," he supplied.

She laughed. "Sometimes, but I know you'll always do what's right, like you did with Irwin and the others. Aren't you pleased with them? With how they are maturing? Yours was a good plan, Caleb. To have them fill their spare time with useful deeds instead of mischief."

"I credit you with any good I've done with those boys," he said to Rebecca. "It might have been my idea, but I doubt I'd have had the courage to follow through if you hadn't seen the value in it."

She snuggled closer to him. "Didn't I just say we made a good pair?" she teased. "You're too modest by half. And if I've made a passable preacher's wife, it's because you've been there every step of the way, holding me up." It wasn't like Caleb to open his heart to her, but she didn't need words to know that he loved her. Anyone who said that marriage was easy wasn't being honest, but she loved Caleb more tonight than she had on the day they'd pledged their vows to each other.

It was as cold as it had been on the previous Christmas Eve when he'd asked her to be his wife, but tonight there was no snow. The stars were bright against a velvet sky, and the horse's breaths made white puffs in the frosty air. She loved the familiar rhythm of the buggy wheels and the animal's hooves on the road. "I was hoping for a white Christmas."

"No snow in sight," Caleb answered. He'd turned into their lane. "There's something for you in the barn. Thought I'd give it to you tonight and leave Christmas morning for Amelia."

Rebecca sat up straight. "But you've already given me this beautiful scarf and new mittens."

"Snow boots for you under the bed. Fur lined, just for around the house. Wouldn't do for church. Not *plain* enough for—"

"For a preacher's wife?" she finished. They laughed together.

"Can't have you with wet feet, can I? Delaware doesn't get much snow, but we're good for rain and mud in winter."

"We are that," she agreed. "But you shouldn't have spent any more money on me. You've already hired Verna Beachy to come three days a week to help me with the housework."

"Made sense. You're doing more and more of my accounts for the wood-carving business. Not to mention the time you spend visiting those in need in the community. But I thought something else would come in handy." He drove to the barn and reined in the horse by the wide double doors. "Come see what I have in here," he said. He helped Rebecca down and then went around to open the back doors. One small daughter, one small dog and one bigger one spilled out. The dogs barked and the girl giggled.

"I didn't tell, Dat," Amelia said. "I kept the secret."

"What secret?" Rebecca asked.

Caleb tied the horse to the hitching rail, took a battery lantern from the buggy and led the way into the stable. Rebecca and Amelia followed him past the empty stall, past where the cow was penned, to the last stall in the row. A sorrel mare with a white nose and a white blaze on her forehead hung her head over the railing.

"You bought a new horse?" Rebecca cried, going close enough to stroke the mare's head. "She's beautiful. What's her name?"

"Daisy. And she's not mine." He grinned at her. "She's—"

"Yours!" Amelia squealed. "Dat bought her for you. And she has a cart!"

"For me?" Rebecca cried. "Oh, Caleb, thank you." She flung herself into his arms and hugged him. "I love her, but why do I need a horse and cart?"

"So you can come and go as you see fit," he answered. "Bishop Atlee said you were busy enough to need your own transportation, and I asked Charley to keep his eyes open for a likely prospect." He stroked the horse's nose. "She's six years old, traffic wise and has no bad habits so far as I can see. Merry Christmas, Rebecca."

"Merry Christmas, Mam!" Amelia echoed.

Tears clouded Rebecca's eyes. This man… This child… This farm and this wonderful present… How could any woman ask for more? She caught Caleb's broad hand and squeezed it tightly. "I love you," she declared. "I love both of you!"

Amelia beamed and snatched up a handful of hay to feed Daisy. Daintily, the mare nibbled at the timothy.

"Come to think of it, I have a gift for you, too, Caleb." Rebecca raised a finger to her lips, and when he bent his head to hear, she whispered her secret into his ear.

A broad grin split his face, and the light from the lantern reflected in his eyes. "When?"

"Late July or early August," she murmured. "Merry Christmas, Caleb."

Laughing, Caleb swung Amelia up into his arms and enveloped both her and Rebecca in a big hug. And in that instant, there was no place else in the world that Rebecca would rather be.

* * * * *

Dear Reader,

Welcome to the Delaware Old Order Amish Community of Seven Poplars, and to the Yoder family and their friends and neighbors. I'm so happy to have you here. Whether you're an old friend to the HANNAH'S DAUGHTERS series or with me for the first time, a place at the kitchen table is always waiting. There are Christmas cookies baking in the oven and hot tea to warm your insides. Take a seat at the table or curl up in the rocking chair and join in the fun. This time, it is daughter Rebecca who risks her heart in an upside-down courtship with the new preacher.

Caleb, scarred by the tragedy that took the life of his first wife, has come to Kent County to start over. But Caleb's brusque manner and his willful young daughter's mischievous ways have driven away one housekeeper after another. When Rebecca accepts the challenge, trouble follows. Everyone agrees that it's time Caleb put the past behind him and remarry, but no one—including the prospective bridegroom—believes lighthearted Rebecca is the right woman for him. And when Rebecca decides that there's more to Caleb than meets the eye, the plot thickens. Opposites attract, or do they?

Wishing you peace and joy in this holiday season,

Emma Miller

Questions for Discussion

1. Among the Old Order Amish, a preacher is usually chosen by lot, for life. Can you see why Caleb would be shocked and daunted by his position? Do his feelings of inadequacy for failing to save his first wife from the fire add to his worry that he wasn't the right man for the job?

2. Caleb was left scarred by the tragedy, but his most serious scars are inside. Do you think that his appearance made him unwilling to consider a popular and attractive girl such as Rebecca to court?

3. What traits did Rebecca see in Caleb that attracted her to him as a prospective husband?

4. Why was Rebecca able to make a connection to Amelia when the earlier babysitters had failed? Do you think Rebecca and Amelia are alike in many ways?

5. What kind of father is Caleb? Do you think he spoils Amelia? Most Amish parents demand obedience from young children. Do you think that Caleb allows Amelia to act out because she lost her mother?

6. Rebecca's beloved younger sister Susanna is a person with mental disabilities. Despite that, do you think that Susanna has more potential for independence than her family realizes?

7. Why did Caleb allow himself to be manipulated into considering marriage to Dorcas?

8. Why was Rebecca's mother worried about Rebecca? Do you believe Hannah's solution of sending her away for a few months was the best one? Why did Rebecca agree?

9. Why do you think that the Amish elders believe that misbehavior by their youth reflects on the entire community? Why do you think they prefer to handle such matters without involving police or social agencies?

10. The Old Order Amish have no health insurance. Do you think this makes them more reluctant to seek health care in emergencies?

11. The majority of Old Order Amish women marry in their early twenties. Marriage is considered a building block of family and faith. Can you understand why Dorcas considered marriage to Caleb despite the lack of chemistry between them? Can you understand why Caleb would consider Dorcas?

12. How did Rebecca's confidence in Caleb change his opinion of himself?

REQUEST YOUR FREE BOOKS!

2 FREE INSPIRATIONAL NOVELS
PLUS 2 FREE MYSTERY GIFTS

Love Inspired

YES! Please send me 2 FREE Love Inspired® novels and my 2 FREE mystery gifts (gifts are worth about $10). After receiving them, if I don't wish to receive any more books, I can return the shipping statement marked "cancel." If I don't cancel, I will receive 6 brand-new novels every month and be billed just $4.74 per book in the U.S. or $5.24 per book in Canada. That's a saving of at least 21% off the cover price. It's quite a bargain! Shipping and handling is just 50¢ per book in the U.S. and 75¢ per book in Canada.* I understand that accepting the 2 free books and gifts places me under no obligation to buy anything. I can always return a shipment and cancel at any time. Even if I never buy another book, the two free books and gifts are mine to keep forever.

105/305 IDN F47Y

Name _____ (PLEASE PRINT)

Address _____ Apt. #

City _____ State/Prov. _____ Zip/Postal Code

Signature (if under 18, a parent or guardian must sign)

Mail to the Harlequin® Reader Service:
IN U.S.A.: P.O. Box 1867, Buffalo, NY 14240-1867
IN CANADA: P.O. Box 609, Fort Erie, Ontario L2A 5X3

**Are you a subscriber to Love Inspired books
and want to receive the larger-print edition?
Call 1-800-873-8635 or visit www.ReaderService.com.**

* Terms and prices subject to change without notice. Prices do not include applicable taxes. Sales tax applicable in N.Y. Canadian residents will be charged applicable taxes. Offer not valid in Quebec. This offer is limited to one order per household. Not valid for current subscribers to Love Inspired books. All orders subject to credit approval. Credit or debit balances in a customer's account(s) may be offset by any other outstanding balance owed by or to the customer. Please allow 4 to 6 weeks for delivery. Offer available while quantities last.

Your Privacy—The Harlequin® Reader Service is committed to protecting your privacy. Our Privacy Policy is available online at www.ReaderService.com or upon request from the Harlequin Reader Service.

We make a portion of our mailing list available to reputable third parties that offer products we believe may interest you. If you prefer that we not exchange your name with third parties, or if you wish to clarify or modify your communication preferences, please visit us at www.ReaderService.com/consumerchoice or write to us at Harlequin Reader Service Preference Service, P.O. Box 9062, Buffalo, NY 14269. Include your complete name and address.

LI13R

SPECIAL EXCERPT FROM

Love Inspired

Bygones's intrepid reporter is on the trail of the town's
mysterious benefactor. Will she succeed in her mission?

Read on for a preview of
COZY CHRISTMAS
by Valerie Hansen, the conclusion to
THE HEART OF MAIN STREET series.

Whitney Leigh rolled her eyes. "Romance! It's getting to
be an epidemic."

Because she was alone in the car, she didn't try to temper her frustration. Fortunately, this time, the editor of the
Bygones Gazette had assigned her to write a new series
about the Save Our Streets project's six-month anniversary.
If he had asked her for one more fluff piece on recent
engagements, she would have screamed.

Parking in front of the Cozy Cup Café, she shivered and
slid out.

As a lifelong citizen of Bygones, she was supposed to
have been perfect for the job of ferreting out the hidden
facts concerning the town's windfall. Too bad she had failed.
Instead of an exposé, she'd ended up filling her column
with news of people's love lives. But she was not going to
quit investigating. No, sir. Not until she'd uncovered the
real facts. Especially the name of their secret benefactor.

She stepped inside the Cozy Cup.

"What can I do for you?" Josh Smith asked.

Whitney was tempted to launch right into her real reason
for being there. Instead, she merely said, "Fix me something warm?"

"Like what?"

"Surprise me."

She settled herself at one of the tables. There was something unique about this place. And, truth to tell, the same went for the other new businesses on Main. Each one had filled a need and become an integral part of Bygones in a mere five or six months.

Josh Smith was a prime example. He was what she considered young, yet he had quickly won over the older generations as well as the younger ones.

He stepped out from behind the counter with a steaming cup in one hand and a taller, whipped-cream-topped tumbler in the other.

"Your choice," he said pleasantly, placing both drinks on the table and joining her as if he already knew this was not a social call.

"I see you're not too busy this afternoon. Do you have time to talk?"

"I always have time for my favorite reporter," he said.

"How many reporters do you know?"

"Hmm, let's see." A widening grin made his eyes sparkle. "One."

Will Whitney get her story and find love in the process?

Pick up COZY CHRISTMAS to find out.
Available December 2013
wherever Love Inspired® Books are sold.